Love Lasts
Forever...

Love Lasts Forever...
only if you don't marry your love

Vikrant Khanna

Srishti
PUBLISHERS & DISTRIBUTORS

SRISHTI PUBLISHERS & DISTRIBUTORS
N-16, C. R. Park
New Delhi 110 019
editorial@srishtipublishers.com

First published by
Srishti Publishers & Distributors in 2014

Typeset by Eshu Graphic

Dedicated to my wife.
Thank you for letting me write
a book on this topic.

Acknowledgements

Thank you friends and family for your love and support. Wify for patiently listening to the story and letting me write it.

Purnima and Samrin for you feedback.
Wasim for the wonderful cover.
Team Srishti.
Swati and Rakesh of Brannia for the branding of my book.

And lastly, thank you readers for picking up this book. I sincerely hope you enjoy reading the story as much as I enjoyed writing it.

PART ~ 1

1. TODAY,

25th June 2011, Transiting Indian Ocean

'And then what happened?' I have never been so intrigued with someone else's story. And that too, a love story of a fifty year old man.

I glance at our Captain. Tears well up in his eyes and he finds it difficult to speak. He doesn't reply and there is a morose look on his face. I notice a gentle quiver in his stance, and I understand. He hasn't completed his story and tells me that the worse is still to come. What can be worse, I wonder. I mean getting a divorce from your childhood sweetheart just a few months after marriage is tragic enough.

Captain Shekhar is tall and sturdily built, but it is his brooding eyes that demand all the attention. Until today I hadn't known that his plaintive love story and loss were shielded by them. For the last few days that I've known him, they were masked behind that dimpled smile which rarely deserted his face.

He looks fit for his age and is mostly bald with some hair left over the sides and the back of his head. With his personality I can be sure he'd have been handsome in his youth.

Pensively he looks ahead from our steaming ship *Adriatic Wave* toward a sight that is quintessential of a beautiful evening. The moon is full and over a million stars gleam from above us, shining and lending their luminosity to the late evening sky which is predominantly clear. The dark grey water below bathes in the ivory hue of the moon. There is a light breeze which adds to the serenity of the Indian Ocean.

'Ronit, do you see something ahead on the horizon, perhaps fine on the starboard bow,' the Captain asks me, wiping his moist eyes, 'a boat maybe?' A stark hollowness has understandably crept into his voice.

I pick up the binoculars and adjust my vision through them. Frankly I am so much caught up in his story that I am hardly interested.

'No, sir,' I reply nonchalantly, 'probably a low altitude star.' I was hardly looking.

I want to know more, dwell deeper into his heart. I want to know why even after the divorce with his wife some three decades ago, he is still madly in love with her.

I presume he is crazy, like all other ship Captains are, particularly at the age of fifty. After spending more than half of their life at sea, all these guys are left with is poignant thoughts. I mean how else can one love someone forever?

And he hasn't even seen her in the past thirty years.

I am this ship's first officer or chief mate as the Europeans like to call me, the first in command to my Captain. We are loaded with almost fifty thousand tons of crude oil loaded from 'Reliance Jamnagar Marine Terminal' located in the Gulf of Kutch in Sikka port in Gujarat. Our discharge port is Immingham in the United Kingdom – a two weeks voyage. But that never worries us; it is the transit through the 'Gulf of Aden' – a piracy infested area near Somalia - that scares the living daylights out of all seafarers.

Now most of you would have just read about these stories in newspapers or probably watched them on TV, a reporter regurgitating the breaking news with the slightest of emotions about Indian seafarers being held captive by the pirates. But if you were here, with us on this ship, you would have started feeling the tremors right at the onset of the voyage.

Here on the bridge – the place from where a ship is navigated – the atmosphere is pretty tense. I mean who would want to be in the captivity of these inhumane people for months or even years. Although personally, I don't think I'll mind too much. At least that would ensure I won't see my wife Aisha for that long.

Getting married was the worst decision of my life; to her, worse than worst. We were in love for seven years before making that horrible decision and since then our love has been nose diving. And now I hate that bitch. Barely a month into our marriage and I could sense her true colours. It now seems to me that she married me only for my money. I have decided to divorce her after I complete my tour of three months here.

With a shake of my head, I try concentrating on the job at hand, and ensure absolutely no suspicious boat hovers around our ship or approaches us. That could be *them*. I look at my Captain; he doesn't look interested in talking anymore and is staring at the radar screen – to get an early warning of any approaching boat.

'Do you see that Ronit,' Captain says, pointing toward a white light which is barely visible over the horizon. 'That is the same light I showed you some time back. It has come close to us now and I sense something fishy. That ship or whatever it is has been changing its speed frequently. I wonder what it is up to.'

Yeah whatever!

I am least interested really. It has been just a couple of weeks since I joined this ship and I can still not get over my wife's taunts. *Where did all the love disappear?* Perhaps my school friend Joe was right by dissuading me to get married. 'Men and women are not meant to co-exist,' he'd reiterate. I always thought that was a quote from some Hollywood flick, but never figured out which one. Only now after our marriage I have found sense in that line.

I see the Captain panicking a bit as he wobbles about his toes, pacing up and down the bridge. I look ahead. There are two lights on either side of the ship – port and starboard in marine terminology. Both the lights are bright now as opposed to the faint image a while earlier. And they are close to us, pretty close. Baffled, I look at my Captain who himself appears vexed. I can bet he has the same question in his head as I have, 'From where the hell did this second boat appear?' There is something terribly fishy happening now. I brush away the thoughts of Aisha.

'Hey Ronit! This boat on our left!' Captain says, pointing toward it in an uncharacteristic shriek. 'It has just lit their light. It was dark all this while. What are these people up to?'

He scampers outside to the bridge wings to get a better picture.

I am up on my feet now. Both the boats are just about two nautical miles from us. The Captain comes running inside shouting *Emergency* and raises an alarm. He orders hard-a-starboard to turn the ship to the extreme right, away from the boats. But as soon as he says it, we watch in horror as both the boats ahead suddenly come close to us, and the next moment are alongside. The pirates employed their age old technique of boarding ships. Two boats are tied with thick hawsers or rope that is underwater so the navigating officer on the ship has absolutely no clue about their collusion, and when the ship touches the hawser, automatically with the ship's momentum, the hawser is pushed ahead and the two boats come alongside.

It is game over for us now. It's a macabre sight to see the pirates launching hooks and rope ladders up our ships' railings and in minutes there are more than a dozen of them onboard.

Two minutes later, three armed pirates enter the bridge and place a gun on the Captain's forehead.

'Your ship is hijacked Captain,' the taller of the three pirates sneers.

2. GRADUATION DAY
February 2004, Mumbai

It was a splendid morning in Mumbai – clear blue skies, crisp sunshine, and a gentle breeze. The day felt even better as after almost a year of rigorous training our batch was finally passing out. The crazy schedule - getting up at four every morning, doing PT exercise in those embarrassing white shorts that flexed our scrotum, and then working and studying till eleven every night - was finally getting over. We were thrilled to say the least.

T.S. Rahaman, our pre-sea training institute, is located at the head of the navigational channel of Mumbai Harbour, on the mainland of Nhava. It boasts of a twenty-two acre lush green and beautiful campus with a sea front on the north west of Nhava. Every day in the past one year, we had regretted our decision of joining the merchant navy. The proverbial 'Life at sea is tough' had made sense to us now.

As we woke up in the morning in our measly room, both of us – Joe and I – had a wide smile on our face, actually, Joe Singh and I.

I'd always found it very outlandish for a Sikh to be named Joe. Despite that, right since our school days, I'd been calling him Joe Singh. I always thought it was more fun that way.

Joe Singh is sturdily built, dark and I always thought being a serd, he is sort of handsome. From the early days that I'd known him, he'd always been easy going and carried himself with aplomb. Friends for more than a decade, we'd first met at a school in Delhi. Joe Singh's uncle was a Captain, earned loads of money, travelled all over the world and bought properties in Mumbai every year. It was pretty much then both of us had made an irrevocable decision of joining the navy.

And after spending a year, we learnt that money was the primary reason that drove all others in our batch to this profession.

Our batch boasted of one hundred and twenty cadets. Needless to say all of us were very excited today. We would finally begin our career with our pre-sea certificates that would guarantee us a place on a ship. And that's when our wages would start. On this note, I quite liked my job. I mean, no other profession offers such high salaries to eighteen year olds, and that too, in American dollars.

'Finally,' Joe Singh gasped. 'We'll be out of here. I'm going to buy a cell phone for myself from my first salary.'

'Good for you,' I said, ironing my uniform.

Our door squeaked open. It was Priyank Bhatia - our neighbour and class monitor.

'Hurry guys, Shukla *ji* is waiting for the fall-in.'

His characteristic cackle irritated the hell out of us. What sort of a guy has a name 'Priyank'! He was much better off with an 'a' at the end of his name. He anyway was a woman trapped in a man's body. Our entire batch, along with the seniors loved pulling his leg, and well, I hate to admit, ogling at him. His rhetoric, voice, gait, stance, and every damn organ of his body screamed femininity. Fair, soft and smooth-skinned, he was like an oasis in a desert full of boys. In the last one year we'd perhaps seen just about half a dozen women on our campus and they were no match to Priyanka's beauty.

Which explains the attraction toward her, I mean him.

'Yes darling, we'll be there in a while,' Joe Singh said with a flying kiss, thrusting his lips toward him.

Priyanka pouted, brandished his arms, and hurriedly moved on to the other rooms. He took his job of a class monitor damn seriously.

'Oh thank God,' I said. 'I'm so glad we'll be out of this shitty place today. I'm longing for the sight of a beautiful woman. It's been ages now.'

'Didn't you just see Priyanka?' snapped Joe Singh.

Half an hour later we queued up in the fall-in. I completely abhorred the idea. It was basically making all the cadets stand in a line like donkeys and a head count was taken to ensure no one was missing. And if at all someone *was* missing, you know, may be due to a drink too many the previous night or a fitful sleep, he had to run the entire length of the campus thrice. That was three kilometers times three, making it a mighty nine kilometers.

Today, however, each one of us had turned up on time for the fall-in. After all, it was the last one.

After the fall-in, we proceeded to a bigger ground where the passing out ceremony was planned amidst huge pomp and show. With over fifteen acres of space, the ground could easily accommodate the families of all the cadets, our instructors and professors. We were made to stand in three groups, with each group comprising of four rows of ten cadets each. In front of us, our families sat and scoured the three groups in search of their lone donkey.

The ceremony began with the dean giving an incumbent speech that was outright boring and horrendous. I mean, come on, you don't scare the cadets who haven't been out at sea by talking about storms and hurricanes that gulp the entire ship within minutes, or blabbering about some nonsensical ghost stories on ships that you experienced, or talk about pirates hijacking ships. All ten minutes that our dean spoke was meant to discourage us from joining shipping. The sixty-something dean invoked a certain amount of terror in our minds that was needless. We would anyway be leaving our families and country for months together. As if that wasn't terror enough. Nevertheless, all of us applauded as the dean left, more out of relief than appreciation.

The ceremony continued with speeches from three more Captains who were the dean's protégés. It was nothing else but another fifteen minutes of sulking under the sun in 'attention' position. Our instructor Shukla *ji* who stood ahead of us between the three groups didn't even have the courtesy to call for a 'stand at ease' position.

I glanced at Joe Singh who appeared equally spent and forlorn and all others, except, of course, Priyanka. He had a bright smile on his face, a smile that was synonymous with pride and honour. I wondered why. Everyone who came here, no matter how lame, would manage to graduate with flying colours. Then why the whole dramatic nod and flattery to every customary sentence churned out by our Captains?

Priyanka had been the most pretentious person I'd known in my entire life. Also, he always *had* to be the best and excel in whatever he did, perhaps, to make up for his feminine image.

Then be that in studies, completing his assignments, finishing his meals, waking up in the morning, reporting for the fall-in, the list was endless. He had this relentless urge to be ahead of everyone which was one of the reasons all of us hated him. The smug look on his face on the day of results was another. And as if that wasn't reason enough, he'd top in all the subjects in all the exams.

Obviously, for being on all fours, genuflecting to all our professors and instructors got him to that position. But nobody gave two hoots about scoring ranks here; all we wanted was that elusive pre-sea certificate that would guarantee us a job on a ship. Ranks never really mattered, but this basic sense always eluded Priyanka.

After the applause that marked the end of all the odious speeches, it was time for the rankings. Top five among us would be given a 'Certificate of Merit' which had no value or meaning. I could sense from a distance Priyanka's head rise a few notches in anticipation of the first prize. A victorious smile unleashed from his face even before the announcement of the results. He appeared so sure he'd get it. I hate to admit but even I was sure about it and so were all others in our batch. He cocked his head toward his family on his right and their hands were already together. I could faintly see in the distance his parents and probably his sister.

As expected, his name was announced as topper of the 2004 batch. A huge round of applause filled the ground and his sister or whoever she was, frisked all over her seat. I felt like killing the bitch.

He marched toward the makeshift stage where the dean waited to honour his wisest donkey. Shukla *ji* began his rant at the top of his voice – 'Left, right, left; left, right, left.'

Priyanka's over-exaggerated, over-enthusiastic, over-dramatic march unleashed a smile on our face. *Seriously dude, get a life!*

And just the next very moment, I heard a huge guffaw of laughter. I looked ahead in the direction of our pretty batch mate and it was the best sight in the world. Priyanka was lying on the ground after tumbling flat on his face. Some people came forward to assist him. I couldn't see his face though, but his crisp white uniform (that once was) was smeared with mud and was a velvety brown colour. His sister's hands were over her mouth in disbelief. Slowly, Priyanka got up on his feet, and uncomfortably wobbled toward the stage.

And that, unquestionably, had to be the most delightful moment of my entire stay here in the past one year.

Over lunch, I met Joe Singh's and some of my other batch mates' parents. Joe Singh nodded toward Priyanka who was busy gorging on his food with his family, just few benches across us in the huge dining hall. He seemed to be in hurry; he had to come first after all. We high-fived at the sight of his hair and uniform that were in complete disarray.

'Come Ronit, let's have some fun.' He strode off toward our pretty batch mate.

'Sure, I love fun.' I padded behind him.

Looking back the past one year, I'd come to realize that I loved fun, especially when it involved Priyanka. Just a few days after we'd joined this institute, everyone had developed an aversion for him, which is what provoked all of us to harass her, I mean him.

I still remember one night, we (Joe Singh and I) tip toed to his room while he was asleep, undid his pyjamas, and then well, his panty (yes panty - it was a baby pink colour with cute little bunnies all over). Joe Singh had tooth paste in his hands which he brought close to Priyanka's butt while I held a torch in my hand, and man, was it clean. There wasn't even a single strand of hair...over there, and for a moment, just a very small moment, I thought I got an erection. Joe Singh placed the tip of the tooth paste over his anus and squeezed it bottom to top generously till it covered the entire area.

'Now we'll see how this slut is the first to report at the fall-in tomorrow,' Joe Singh whispered in my ear.

And then, just the way we came, we tip-toed our way out the room.

The next morning was complete hysteria as he hollered and pranced all over the bathroom floor with a hand over his butt.

'Ooh, aah, urgh, who the hell has put this paste?' he screamed. 'Oh God, this is burning like hell.'

All of us laughed our lungs out.

'Who has done this? I'll complain to Shukla *ji*.'

He kept whining but no one paid a heed. Although everyone knew it was us, but no one took our name. By the way, he also knew it was us, we also knew he knew that it was us, but we also knew that he knew that nobody would support him.

At the fall-in, Priyanka was late as expected as he spent a major chunk of his time in...well, cleaning his ass. And then the best part to top it all – he got punished. So with his clammy butt he ran nine kilometres. Watching him suffer like that gave us a lot of pleasure.

And yes, Shukla *ji* didn't buy his bull shit: 'Don't give excuses Priyank, no one can do such a morbid thing, we are all officers here. Learn to accept your mistake.'

Divine pleasure!

And then another time, we'd stolen his shore pass. Once in a month we'd get a holiday in form of a pass to leave our institute in the Nhava Island via a boat to see Mumbai. It was anybody's guess that Joe Singh and I stole his pass not once but thrice. So while all of us spent the entire day away from the confined atmosphere in Nhava Island and enjoyed sightseeing in Mumbai, Priyanka darling was confined to the four walls of his room shedding tears. Yes, he cried. Again we knew that he knew it was us. And so on.

So yeah, when Joe Singh calls me to have fun, I am all game for it.

'Hey Priyank, congrats for the prize,' Joe Singh said as we reached his table. 'You had a nasty fall there.' His tone was borderline sarcastic.

I pursed my lips and pinched him from behind.

Priyanka nodded stoically and introduced us to his parents. We knew he hated us from the bottom of his heart. Of course, the feelings were reciprocated. We checked out the odd pattern of mud formed over his shirt. *Why the hell was he not bleeding?*

'Hi, I'm Aisha, Priyank's sister.' A perky voice greeted us from behind a minute later.

When I turned, the prettiest pair of eyes on this planet twinkled at me.

I gaped at her in amazement and felt a hundred needles run up the back of my neck. My heart did a little dance and my eyes were locked in hers. Beyond her, the entire world was out of focus.

I'm in love. Oh man, I'm so in love.

3. PIRATES

25th June 2011, Somewhere in Somalia

My thoughts about my graduation day overwhelm me with grief and guilt. Why did I join the navy? And more importantly why did I meet Aisha that day?

As I traverse back in reality, I still can't get over the shock. *The pirates have hijacked our ship...*It's been less than an hour since the pirates boarded and they have already taken command of our ship. There are at least a dozen of them with us on the bridge and another dozen all around. The skiffs or boats through which they boarded were actually launched by a mother ship some few nautical miles away from us. No wonder neither me, nor Captain, could figure out from where the two boats appeared. The lone white light that we saw first was of the mother ship itself. And then the two lights were of the boats. So by that time, the mother ship had switched off her lights to catch another prey.

After boarding they asked us to approach their mother ship from where another dozen of pirates boarded so as to be in complete control. All the pirates are armed with sophisticated and modern day weapons viz. RPGs and AK-47s. The Somalis are insanely dark and ghoulish looking people. Even if it wasn't for their guns, I wouldn't mess with them. Most of them are lanky but some of them are stout and massive built. However they all invoke the same amount of terror. I remember the speech of our dean during my pre-sea days some seven years ago. He was so darn right. We are living the most dreaded day of any seafarer's life.

As soon as they entered the bridge, they told the Captain to follow their route in a smattering of English. Their accent was hard to place, both of us pressed hard. Later, the Captain and I studied their route carefully. They were taking us in a south westerly direction to some port in Mogadishu, Somalia's capital. No one amongst us uttered a word in retaliation. We knew its outcome. A bullet!

Two decks below, all our ship's crew members, some twenty-five of them, have been assembled in the small mess room. They have been made to sit on the floor with the pirates strategically positioned around them, guns in their hands, with orders of shoot if any one moves.

Here on the bridge, the atmosphere is relatively safe. Of course the 'shoot orders' apply here as well but they are a bit wary about it as they need us, at least till the time we get there. The pirates are not good navigators and have a limited knowledge of bridge equipments; they lack essential radio communication skills as well to communicate with their partners ashore. So till the time we reach their desired location, we are pretty much in safe hands.

Till the time we reach we are safe!

My own thought has managed to send a shiver down my spine and props up disconcerting questions in my head.

What would happen after that? Would they kill us? Would they torture us till we are dead? Will we ever be out of their custody?

4. OUR FIRST DATE
February 2004, Mumbai

Barely twenty-four hours into our first meeting, and here I was, already, on a date with Priyank's sister Aisha.

After a cursory visit to the 'Gateway of India' we made our way to the Italian joint 'Pizzazz' in Mumbai's up market Marine drive area overlooking the Arabian Sea. As we entered, we caught an intoxicating whiff of hot dough and mozzarella cheese, and it was the most amazing smell. There was a rustic ambience about the place, and I couldn't see many unoccupied tables. The walls were adorned by posters of Hollywood stars, and some of them, I noticed, were peeling off from the edges. Western rock music blared from the speakers toward the left of the table we settled in.

As she checked out the menu dithering on what to order, I checked *her* out. I must admit that I was completely blown over by her beauty yesterday, and today, she looks even prettier than I remembered.

From the very little that I have known her, I would best describe her as someone with an understated elegance and a charming personality that oozes confidence and grace. She isn't tall, a few inches over five feet perhaps, has thin golden brown hair, immaculately manicured hands, and smooth white skin like Priyank. With blue jeans complimented by a flowery mustard top and the slightest hint of make-up, she managed to look sensual.

I was so inundated by her beauty yesterday that I ditched Joe Singh to have lunch with Priyank's family. He's not 'Priyanka' by the way; I have stopped calling him that. After all, he's my future brother-in-law, he deserves some respect now.

Yes, I have decided to marry Aisha some day in the future. Love changes us all, doesn't it?

Yesterday, over lunch, we sat across each other and invariably I noticed her checking me out from the corner of her eyes. I felt a knot tighten in my stomach and sensed something skeptical. I smiled incredulously at her and wondered how on earth a beautiful woman like her could get attracted to me. Maybe her brother had told her about us, how we tease him and all that, and she'd decided to teach me a lesson.

But as sense dawned, I realized I was decent enough to attract pretty women after all. Closing in at six feet with sinewy body and chiselled features, I too was a catch for her. That's when I decided to ask her out.

While bidding adieu to Priyank's family and hugging him dramatically pretending how much I would miss him, I offered Aisha a *nice meeting you* hand shake passing her a little note scribbled over a tissue paper:

I don't know if I've been searching for true love,
Or waiting for it to come knocking at my door,
But the moment I've rested my eyes on you,
I've found what I've been looking for, and never want to let it go.

Tomorrow, 5pm, Churchgate.

She cast a furtive glance at the paper at once, rolled her eyes quickly through my words, and then deftly nodded her head with her eyes twinkling in unison. I almost screamed in excitement.

'Why did you call me here?' she asked, looking up from the menu, as though oblivious of the reason.

I rolled my eyes and exhaled sharply. Now that is something I hate in a woman. Why do they have to pretend they are dumb? And why do they think *we* are dumb?

OK, if that's what she wants, here's the answer:

'Because I love you,' I replied unfazed, looking straight into her eyes. I really did. I had only heard about love at first sight, but yes it happens.

'What?' She sort of snorted throwing the menu at the table. She still couldn't decide what to order. 'You can't love me, you barely know me,' she declared.

'Yes, I really do,' I said, taking her hand in mine.

I knew I appeared a bit in a hurry, but I had no choice. I'd be leaving for my first ship next month for the next six months, and I didn't want to wait that long to convey my feelings to her. Besides beauties like her have a very limited span of availability.

She blushed. Gracefully, she withdrew her hands from mine, and a faint smile engulfed her face.

'You're so bad,' she drawled, tucking her hair behind her ears.

'I am,' I chuckled, leaning back in my seat. *Was that a yes?*

She cleared her throat, handed me the menu, and we ordered. During food we chatted on inane topics and contemplated life. She thrust her brother in our conversation from nowhere and that's when I almost threw up.

'Priyank is such a sweet lad, isn't he?' I saw a gleeful spark in her eyes as she dug her fork in the pasta. 'I mean he is the sunshine of our life, he's so competitive and full of energy; no one can beat him in *anything*. He's just *the best*.'

'I can't agree more,' I replied non-commit-tally, looking everywhere else but in her eyes.

Sweet lad?

'Isn't it?' She adjusted herself on the seat and moved closer to me. The exuberance in her expression was disconcerting. 'You know my whole life revolves around my brother. He is my best friend, my mentor, in fact he is everything to me other than a brother.'

'Really? Wow!' I held the glass of Pepsi and took a long sip. The brother-sister talk brought tears to my eyes, well almost. Not due to affection, of course, but due to fear. Did she even know how much her beloved brother hates me and Joe Singh, and likewise?

'Does Priyank know you are em...here with me?' I asked, hoping for an outright no.

'No, I haven't told him yet...' she replied almost instantly while chewing her food along.

Thank God! I breathed a sigh of relief.

'...And I've been feeling guilty about it all this while.'

She looked wistfully out of the window. I followed her gaze. The sun was slowly beginning its descent down the horizon. The sky was orange, and the sea glistened in gold, reflecting its colour. In the distance, dusk was slowly making its way over.

'You know' - she scooted her head over, facing me - 'I never hide anything from him. I think I'm going to tell him about you today. You guys are friends, I'm sure he'll be thrilled by the news.'

'Oh sweetie, you have no idea.' I took a small bite of the garlic bread before dipping it in ketchup.

'What do you mean?' she raised her brow, wiping her lips with a tissue paper.

'Nothing,' I said. 'I just feel this is not the right time to tell him, let's see where we go first. We should take it easy for a while.'

'Yeah, actually, you are right,' she agreed.

Thank God, again!

She took a slow breath. 'He'll be so bamboozled by the news, I mean, you know, you are his friend and all, dating his sister. That might shock him.'

I smiled. 'There you go, sounds about right, SHOCK!'

She nodded. I relaxed my muscles, unclenched my fist, and suddenly air flew more comfortably to my lungs.

But suddenly, a very unnerving question popped up in my head. *What would happen if Priyank tells her about me? Will she kick me or slap me?*

'But you know Ronit,' she resumed in a concerned tone, breaking my thought. 'Priyank tells me there are some rowdy and unethical batch mates of his who are so jealous of him that they've been troubling and ragging him right from the onset of this course. I want to kill those guys.'

'Em...sorry...what?' I preferred pretending I never heard that.

She repeated her statement verbatim but ended with a question, 'Do you know who those guys are?'

'No idea at all, absolutely no idea,' I answered spontaneously and avoided looking in her eyes again.

'I hope those guys rot in hell.'

She said it with so much power and conviction, I was pretty sure Joe Singh and I would actually end up that way.

'Hey look!' I pointed through the window toward a horse cart galloping down the Marine Drive, primarily to change the topic. 'You want a ride later.'

'Love to.'

We left the restaurant an hour later after settling the bill and I ensured Priyank's topic was completely knocked out of her head.

On the ride, as the cool wind of the Arabian Sea blew past our face and caressed us, I looked at her and couldn't help but wonder, how could I possibly be in love with a person so madly, whom I met just yesterday.

5. JOE SINGH'S ADVICE
February 2004, Mumbai

Joe Singh resided in Jalvayu Vihar in Powai; a complex developed by the naval and air force housing board. Although he spent more time in Delhi than Mumbai, he preferred the *Mumbaikar* tag over a *Delhite* one. And I didn't know why, but I hated him for that.

With the morning sun shining nice and bright in the sky, I found myself reaching for his place. After my first date yesterday with the love of my life, I'd been bubbling with excitement to share the news with him. I wanted to see the reaction, or perhaps shock – as Aisha had put it – on his face; hence I decided to meet him in person. Joe Singh's parents left home early so their maid opened the door. Joe Singh once confided in me that he had the hots for her daughter, and well, that was the weirdo in him.

Talking about the 'weirdo in him', he also had a *thing* for Priyank. Correction – a *thing* for his arse. That 'toothpaste night', Joe Singh had brought a camera with him.

And I hated that screensaver on his computer screen. It was there for two months!

Shunning my best friend's thoughts, I approached his room. A poster of 'Rabbi Shergill' and 'Beatles' competed with each other on the wall opposite the bed. The room was tiny yet looked elegant with just the bare minimum furniture - an ebony coloured TV unit, two side tables on each side of the mahogany coloured bed, a wooden attached wardrobe, and two bean bags occupied the side.

Joe Singh's head was buried under the pillow and the blanket slovenly covered his body.

'Wake up you moron, its eleven.' I jostled him.

'Um…' He moaned.

'Get up man, got some interesting stuff to tell you.'

'Um…'

'I was with Aisha yesterday.'

Still nothing.

'Aisha…is…Priyank's…sister,' I drawled to create a dramatic effect.

'Whhaatt?' He threw his blanket and as if like a sorcerer sat beside me the very next moment. 'Who?' he asked; his curled lips and narrowed eyes manifested his curiosity.

'Yes! You heard it right! Aisha, Priyank's sister!'

'Hold on dude,' he cut in, thrusting his arms at me, 'first things first. Since when did you start calling him Priyank? We'd already established he's a girl, right?'

My memory raced back to that night when Joe Singh creamed his butt with toothpaste. The way he screamed in the corridor cavorting all over the place, the way he sobbed, and then didn't speak to anyone for two days after the punishment was enough evidence to establish he was a girl. It appeared as if he was having PMS those days.

And that's when we morphed his name to Priyanka.

'Since I fell in love with his sister,' I replied, traversing back to the present.

'Fell in love…His sister…What are you even saying?' He scrunched up his nose and threw his blanket further away. 'What is wrong with you? Are you completely out of your mind? Had we not established love and marriage is a disaster and we'll stay away from them at least till we are thirty? You can't be falling in love,' he declared.

Again, my memory raced back to that day, few months back, when we were having an innocuous argument with our instructor Shukla *ji* in the mess room. At fifty-five, he was still a bachelor and at the peak of his health. He exhorted us to never get married and live life to the fullest. I still remember his little poem partially that he recited that night. It went something like this:

Seaman life, no wife;
New port, new wife.

That night when Joe Singh and I were back in our room, enthused by Shukla *ji's* words, we made a pact that we won't get married, or at least till we were thirty. Life was meant to be enjoyed after all.

'Yeah, I know dude, I remember.' I took a deep breath, and again, traversed back to reality. 'But love…that's what it does to you; makes you forget everything else and takes you in this world that is wonderfully extra ordinary.'

Joe Singh tutted, rose to his feet, and headed for the washroom.

'I don't believe it,' he called out from inside. 'And what about all that fun we'd planned we'll have together, you know, all that exploring new countries thing, women of different accents, colours, shapes and sizes; remember, it was all part of the plan.'

I poked my head out the window adjacent to his bed. From the fifteenth floor, people appeared the size of ants.

'Now you won't even reply to me or what?' I heard his muffled scream from behind the door.

'I know man, but I'm sorry!' I roared. 'I'm so madly in love with her that I can't even imagine myself with another woman.'

'Oh man, you are so gonna regret this in future.'

He came out with a scowl and started for his wardrobe.

'Are you crazy, love is not meant to be regretted, it is meant to be cherished,' I protested to his back while he was busy rooting for something. 'Being in love is the most marvellous thing that can happen to someone. I am so glad it happened to me. All the other plans mean absolutely nothing. All I want is to be engulfed in this beautiful feeling of love for the rest of my life by getting married to her.'

'Oh really?' He turned round and let out a half-suppressed laugh. 'Men and women are not meant to co-exist with each other. Always remember that!'

'Huh!' I crinkled my nose.

'And *Priyanka's* sister?' He took a step forward and shook his head distastefully. 'Are you crazy? I mean what sort of a family has a son like Priyanka? Oh, Ronit buddy, you are gonna regret this in future big time.'

I gnashed my teeth and glared at him.

What sort of a person is he; he doesn't believe in the magic of love? I mean seriously, what sort of a person is he?

I candidly dismissed his opinion and views about love and my life, and silently patted my back.

6. WHERE ARE WE?
25th June 2011, Somewhere in Somalia

Why did I not listen to him that day? How could he possibly see the future?

Although I am trembling with fear and my heart continues to pound hard against my chest at the gory implications of what the pirates can or may do to us, my mind continues to drift in the past. I am terrified, I'm worried, yet I'm also filled with remorse, melancholy…and anger. Certainly I'd never expected my love story of seven years to tailspin to this low.

I fell in love believing it to be the most marvellous thing that could happen to anyone; if anything, it's the most terrible thing. And marriage, well…from where do I even begin? I firmly believe it's a curse inflicted upon mankind.

I shake my head, hating myself for everything that transpired following our marriage. Inhaling a deep breath, I look around. It's been more than four hours now since these pirates first boarded our ship.

Just then the leader of the pirates orders the Captain to reduce the speed of the ship. It seems we have almost reached. *But where?* I share startled looks with Captain.

Although, whatever had to happen has happened, I secretly wish the pirates had boarded after an hour or so. *At least till Captain had completed his story…*

I never thought love stories like these exist in the real world. He was telling me earlier this afternoon, when we were having a little talk in his cabin, that he has known his wife all his life. They first met at the tender age of eight, fell madly in love few years later, and then got married as teenagers.

Till here, I was with him.

But then later, I lost him as he continued.

What I couldn't discern is with so much love around how could his wife ask for a divorce with minor hiccups here and there just few months after their marriage? Every relationship has its share of problems; she, of all the people should have understood that. And then the Captain signed the divorce papers and threw them at her face.

So then why now, thirty years later, he is still madly in love with her? And if so much for love, why did he not get back with her? What is the worst part that is still to come, he told me before these pirates boarded?

I shoot a brief look at the Captain. He appears lost in thoughts. *Just tell me why?*

My thoughts are interrupted by the bridge door thrown open suddenly. Our cook hobbles in, almost short of breath, and hollers at the top of his voice, 'Captain! Help Captain! Pirates! Please help us!'

The Captain glares at him and purses his lips with a finger on them. Of course, the cook gets the message, but it's a tad too late. The ominous looking leader signals to one of his men who barely nods as I stare in disbelief.

Oh my God! What is he going to do?

Without further ado, the *hit man* impassively brings his gun close to his chest and pulls the trigger. I squeeze my eyes shut and bring my hands to cover my gaping mouth. My heart hammers loudly in my chest as I hear almost half a dozen shots and a loud shriek. All of us freeze in shock and a few hairs rise on my arms and the back of my neck. I fail in the attempt to bring my shaking hands to rest, and flash a brief look over the side. The cook is lying dead on the floor with blood smeared all over the bulkheads of the bridge. I resist the urge to vomit and look at the Captain who is resting his forehead in his palms. From the little that I know him, he is cursing himself for the events that have unfolded this evening.

Two pirates come forward toward the cook's dead body, bend down, and yank at his arms. They trudge toward the bridge wings leaving a trail of blood behind them. Next, we hear a loud splash of water at the cook's body hitting the Arabian Sea.

'Captain! Tell your people to do only what we say and we will not kill anyone else!'

The low and gravelly voice of the leader was almost incomprehensible.

The Captain nods slowly.

About an hour later our ship is stopped and we are surrounded by islands with barren mountains all around. In the distance a few ships are anchored and over a hundred armed pirates are guarding them.

We have reached our destination.

7. OUR FIRST GOODBYE
March 2004, Mumbai

Little more than a month in our relationship and we had to face the toughest part – separation.

I flew down to Mumbai from Delhi especially to meet Aisha, for my final goodbye. I took Joe Singh's car, picked her up from her house in Bandra and we sat on the pavement on Marine Drive gazing ahead toward the Arabian Sea.

Aisha was wearing cream capris and matched it with a blue top. Her hair was tied in a high pony tail with a matching hair band and round earrings dangled from her ears. Even in her simplicity she had to be the prettiest girl I'd seen in my life.

Ahead of us the water swished back and forth, lapping against the rocks and rose in plumes with a few drops directed at us every now and then. There was a light breeze; the intensity of which just perfect that would make one feel that life indeed is wonderful. Behind us, people jogged with headphones on their ears, and further down cars rattled down the noisy Mumbai streets. Not too far from us toward our left there was a *Bollywood* shooting in progress as people appeared to throng the sets. Above us the birds went about with their evening songs, lost in their world. Everything seemed normal with the world, yet for us, nothing was normal.

I would be leaving for my first assignment as a cadet tomorrow for six months…

'Wow!' Aisha gasped. 'I can't believe we met just last month. I'm so much in love with you already Ronit.'

She slipped her arms around me and rested her head on my shoulders.

I sighed. 'I know,' I said, squeezing her petite hands. 'I've just seen you four times and it feels as if I've known you for a lifetime already. I love you so much, Aisha.'

She forced a smile. 'I'll miss you Ronit.'

I could hear her voice breaking. My heart cried at that.

Glumly, I looked ahead in the distance. Faraway, near the horizon, a ship was propelling through the water leaving smoke in its wake. I shuddered to think I'd be on one of those by tomorrow, away from land, away from Aisha, *away from my Aisha…*

Seriously, I had never thought love could be so hard. Staying close to six months away from her would be like an eternity. Just last month I was so excited about my first salary in dollars. And now, all the excitement had vanished in thin air. No amount of money could justify the separation from her.

A few days earlier I had thoughts of quitting the navy so I could spend each and every moment of my life with her. I'd shared this with Joe Singh to take his point of view earlier this afternoon. I had not seen a more astounded look on his face.

'What? You are gonna forget all the shit we have gone through in the past one year?' Joe Singh said in a gruff voice. 'What is happening to you man, get a control over your life.' He tutted before resuming. 'Seriously man love is blind, I mean, one year of struggle and when it's time to earn the reward, you want to quit, and that too for a girl. And Priyanka's sister, for *her*.'

He thumped his fist on the table and had a look of disgust on his face. 'I mean seriously for Priyanka's sister!' And then he began to snigger. 'Priyanka's' sister? Ha, ha, really?'

'Thanks for the advice,' I'd replied with gritted teeth, before stomping out of his house. Not before collecting the keys of his car, of course.

For a minute I wanted to forget Joe Singh's advice and leave my job. My life is so perfect and complete when I am around Aisha. She is the best thing that has ever happened to me.

'What are you thinking Ronit?' she asked, running her fingers playfully over my arms.

I let out a deep breath. 'Nothing much,' I replied with a smile.

I fiddled with a stone and then hurled it across the water feeling the emotions surge within me. I glanced over my shoulder and there were couples as far as my eyes could reach. Some of them hid behind rocks and went about their business while others were content like us to spend a nice, romantic evening in company of the sea.

I wrapped my arms around her shoulders and snuggled closer. The wind had seemed to pick up as the calm sea was suddenly flecked with whitecaps. The sun had left for the day, gulped down by the sea, leaving behind an amber colour in the sky. Soon it would be time for me to leave as well. Then suddenly, out of nowhere, something hit me and I turned to face her, and said, 'Hey, what if we get married now?'

'What? Ha, ha, seriously?' That gleeful spark in her eyes reinstated my decision.

I smiled under my breath. 'Yeah, seriously, what do you say?'

'What?' she snorted. 'Are you crazy? We are just eighteen!'

'I know and that is pretty much the legal age to get married in India; isn't it?'

She hid her face beneath her hands, and shook her head in disapproval, or out of shyness, or contempt, I couldn't really fathom. Then she looked at me, smiled, and said, 'seriously Ronit you want to get married to me at the age of eighteen and that too after knowing me for just about a month!'

'Absolutely! You heard it right,' I said without any thought or hesitation. I was so sure I wanted to marry this girl and spend my life with her. What more can I want? I mean what more can anyone want, being in love and getting married, and all that, right?

'I love you Aisha and where does it say you can't get married at the age of eighteen or after knowing a person for just over a month.'

'Yeah, I know,' she said, 'but…you are being weird.'

'Weird? Why?' I threw a curious look at her. When she had nothing to offer, I asked, 'Alright, will you marry me or not?'

'Of course,' she said, 'I love you and may be we'll get married sometime in the future, but not now, I mean as teenagers. You are anyway leaving tomorrow.'

'Yeah, so what, we'll get married before I leave. I still have a day.'

'OK, now, hold on marriage boy.' She perked up on her seat and freed her arms from mine. 'It's getting creepy now, you please go and come back; we'll date for a few years and then decide if we should even get married in the first place.'

'What? So you have doubts about that now?'

'No,' she said, 'I didn't say that, but I think marriage is not child's play, you have to be sure that you are doing the right thing.' She rolled her eyes. 'And with the right guy...' she whispered under her breath. Her last line wasn't intended to be heard, but she said it a tad too loud.

'So you are not even sure about me now?'

'No! I'm not saying that, I mean, we ought to give ourselves more time Ronit before even thinking of getting married.'

'OK, look, here's the deal. I am sure that I want to get married to you right away, just tell me whenever you are ready and I'll be at your doorstep asking for your hand from your father, and well...brother.'

I only got a wry smile in return.

An hour later I was dropping her home driving past the crazy Mumbai traffic. Silently, I actually admired it. More traffic meant more time with Aisha. She rolled down the window and craned her neck out, enjoying the wind past her face. Her hair flew with the wind like the waves of the ocean.

'I don't believe I'm so madly in love, Ronit,' she said breathily a minute later as she settled back on her seat. 'It feels so good and bad at the same time,' she added in a whisper.

I nudged her shoulder mischievously. 'I want a good bye kiss.'

'There you go! All you men are the same,' she spluttered, moving away from me in her seat. 'I'm trying to have a nice romantic talk here and all you want is a...damn kiss.'

'So what's unromantic about that?' I asked.

She gave me a cold stare. 'You are so bad.'

That definitely was the cue of her approval. 'So we'll do it?'

'No, I can't let you do it,' she replied curtly. 'It's just been a month in our relationship.'

I waited.

'OK, but I will not allow you to kiss me on my lips, only cheeks,' pat came her reply only a minute later. *Why couldn't she admit she wanted it too?*

'OK,' I replied casually, pulling up the car down the road. 'Let's do this.'

'In the car?' she said distastefully.

'Yeah, where else, you want me to get a room for you?'

'You are really bad; I'll never do it here.'

Ten minutes later we had our tongues in each other's mouth, and yes, we did it *in the car.*

While on my way back toward Joe Singh's house to drop his car, I was struck by the realization that today had to be the best day of my life.

8. TEN MILLION DOLLARS
26th June 2011, Somewhere in Somalia

I wish she had refused that elusive kiss, and in frustration, I had killed the bitch. I would have to live in a prison then, but at least, without her. Life here is no less than a prison anyway!

It has been almost a day in the captivity of these inhuman people. All the crew members have been escorted to the bridge and including me and the Captain, have been made to sit on the bridge floor in silence.

In pin drop silence!

I have been sitting in this place, in this position, for more than twelve hours now. We are not allowed to move; they have told they won't harm us if we follow their orders. My legs and back are aching, my knees are knocking and my stomach is growling.

In the morning a group of men had come to assess the ship, the cargo, and the crew to decide on the ransom amount. A representative of the pirates called 'Translator' who was their chief negotiator had accompanied them. He spoke immaculate English and had to be the smartest Somalian around. Together with the leader he decided on a whopping ten million dollars ransom and informed the company with the help of the Captain.

I almost threw up after hearing that amount. With the austerity measures being taken in the shipping industry owing to the recession, I have serious doubts of our release. But the cargo on our ship might just be the saving grace as its value is much more than the ship itself, and well, us.

To further add to my misery, I am grappling to find the answers to the Captain's story.

What is the catch? Is he crazy?

I have been trying to make eye contact with him ever since we reached here so he gives me some hint as to what happened in the end. This is the first time in my life I am more interested in someone else's life story rather than my own. He had told me he wants to help me, so that I don't make the same mistakes he made.

But I don't see any of his mistakes...

It was his stupid wife who was careless and made all the mistakes in their marriage. She was the one who asked for a divorce, not him. Then where the hell is his mistake? Why has he been feeling so guilty for their separation? And more importantly, I can't help but ask myself all the time, 'Why is he still madly in love with her?' In fact, how can one love someone forever? Especially after getting married to that same person?'

I don't have a good control over my mind and it drifts aimlessly from the Captain's story to my own. But what else can I do here anyway?

I wrap my arms around my knees and look around. All of us have a woeful expression and we glance at each other helplessly – in shock, pain, fear. None of us have been able to accept the fact that this has actually happened. The goddamn hijack still seems a nightmare.

Then there is another feeling that's aggravating our misery – hunger. They haven't given us food yet and we haven't eaten anything in the last eighteen hours. I am starving. But honestly if I were to get food cooked by my wife here, I think I'll avoid it. *What does she even cook?* Horrible will be an understatement. And then she tells me I'm a little *ma'ama's boy* who can only enjoy food cooked by his mother. From where does my mother even come in the picture? And why can't two women ever stay peacefully together?

As I struggle to find the answers (which I know I never will), a faint smile has unleashed on everyone's face. Finally the food is here! Not much though, however, enough for us to keep going. The pirates can't let us die; their purpose would not be served otherwise. What bargaining power would they have if all of us were dead?

A few minutes later, I dig into the clammy rice that is served with some awfully looking vegetable served in soiled paper plates thrown at us. I am too hungry to make a face and silently try to eat it. That should be our meal for the next twenty four hours. Horrible as it is, it makes me want to ask the pirates one question ever since the food hit my tongue, 'Did Aisha cook this?'

9. SORRY BROTHER!
July 2007, Mumbai

We'd been dating for over three years now and every year on our anniversary I'd been asking her to marry me. For some reason I never get a coherent answer and she'd always manage to gurgle out something, digressing from the topic of marriage. *Does she even want to get married? To me, more importantly.*

Today, she called me over to her place for a cup of coffee. Her parents and her sister Priyank, I mean brother, were not around. The moment she asked me, I'd been squealing with excitement over the phone with Joe Singh.

'Dude this is it, your night, make it large,' Joe Singh yelped. I couldn't figure out why *he* was that happy.

'Are you thinking what I'm thinking,' I asked him hesitantly. I didn't want to discuss...you know what, about my future wife with my best friend.

'Of course! She has not called you for coffee, that's anybody's guess.' He screamed into the phone.

OK, now seriously, why was *he* so excited?

'Just do it and then tell her to buzz off, your job is done here,' he added malevolently, interrupting my thoughts.

'What? No! I'm not gonna tell her to buzz off!' I snapped.

'How many times have I told you I love her and want to spend the rest of my life with her, Joe Singh?'

'Oh don't you call me that!' he said. 'And how many times have *I* told you to address me as just Joe, it sounds weird that way, man.'

'OK, Joe Singh.'

'Fucker!' he said, giggling. 'You'll never learn, huh? Anyway man, listen. Don't be so much in love with her because you'll get hurt if things don't work out between you two. Trust me man it's not worth it. These girls have a tremendous power to hurt us guys.'

'Oh really!' I said, cradling the phone between my left shoulder and ear, and glancing through my pictures with Aisha taken last year. She looked phenomenally pretty in that navy blue sweater. 'And how could you possibly know that? You've never had a girlfriend man.'

'Just...common sense...that's...all,' he fumbled.

'Bye,' I said hurriedly, 'and please never give me such lame advice again.'

I kept her picture aside and opened my closet to get ready for the evening. My aunt was kind enough to have given me a room in her flat in Andheri whenever I visited Mumbai.

'So how do you like your coffee?' Aisha asked.

She was wearing light blue faded jeans with a bottle green coloured *kurta* that reached her knees. Either she was short or the *kurta* was long. Either ways, she looked ravishing.

'Just the way you like it, sweetie,' I replied, seated on the beige coloured sofa.

Though the flat was small for obvious reasons (Bandra, Mumbai!) it didn't look that small owing probably, to the choice of furniture. The L-shaped sofa sat at the far end of the drawing room saving every inch of the available space. In the middle was a black sliding centre table over a purple rug. Adjoining the drawing room, a six-seated dining table occupied the hallway. To sum it up, the interiors were very tastefully done, and I liked the open kitchen concept. I could almost see her in the kitchen, her back toward me, stirring something.

I rose and waddled toward her. Her hair was open, and almost managed to shroud her back. As I got closer to her, my heart began pounding against my chest. I stopped inches behind her and placed my arms at the side of her hips. She flinched gently and I moved my arms in front, on her belly, and drew her closer. I snuggled close to her and buried my face in her hair, basking in its scent. She placed her arms on mine and I ran my hands slowly over them. She turned round and hugged me, resting her head over my chest. I raised my arms toward her back and hoped this time to pause forever. Slowly, she withdrew her face and tilted it upward to look into my eyes, wrapping her arms around my neck. 'I love you,' she whispered.

Her chirpy voice sent my body in jitters, and I smiled back. 'I love you so much,' I said, leaning closer and kissed her softly on her forehead.

Abruptly, almost surprising me, she moved away from me toward the shelf on our left. She opened it and pulled out a light pink coloured mug. She poured whatever she was stirring in the mug and offered me.

'Coffee, that's why I called you here in the first place.'

'Alright,' I said, 'thanks!'

I almost puked with the very first sip. It had to be the most horrible coffee ever.

'So how's it?' she asked, widening her eyes at me.

'It's amazing, thanks.' Come on, I love her, can't be ruining her mood for a cup of coffee.

'Is it?' she asked sceptically, leaning forward. 'Priyank tells me I make the most horrible coffee in the world.'

And *then* I puked, unable to resist my laughter. I placed the cup aside and yanked her toward me. 'Yes it's horrible; in fact horrible is an understatement.'

And then we both laughed. Thankfully, that didn't upset her.

'So won't you be showing me your house?' I asked in the pretext of sneaking into her bedroom.

'Of course!' She held my hand, tugging at it, and I meekly followed her.

We started with her bedroom. It was spotless and orderly in appearance and there wasn't even a single thing that seemed out of place. There were a bunch of soft toys - some of them, I noted, my gifts to her on our previous dates - neatly arranged on the marble-white chester adjacent to her bed. The glossy white bed was tucked in one corner of the room draped by a flowery pink bed sheet. Behind the bed, the wall was adorned by wallpaper – a delectable assortment of tiny flowers across it – that perfectly matched the purple rug, fuchsia curtains, and the bed sheet. To embellish the room further there were more than a couple of flower vases with well-tended roses and tulips. I couldn't miss the shade of pink in them.

She collected one of her albums from a drawer, and we began leafing through it on her bed. I lifted my hands and tucked the hair over her face behind her ears. Slowly, keeping the album aside, I leaned against her and took my lips closer to hers. She closed her eyes and I followed in quick succession. I felt her soft and pudgy lips on mine and for the next five minutes or so, the world beyond her didn't exist. I gradually slipped my hands down, toward her breasts, and felt them. She made a muffled sound and tried to resist me. I accorded, only to further slide down my hands to remove her *kurta*. Instantly she scrambled away and our kiss ended.

'No Ronit, we are not doing this,' she warned.

'Doing what?' I said.

'You know what, don't act funny with me!' she waggled a finger at me.

'Okay, sorry.' I got up feigning a morose expression and pretended to walk out.

'I mean...um...you know...um...somebody might come,' she spluttered.

There you go. I knew it.

I strode back and sat on the bed beside her. 'No one will come, you yourself said that,' I said encouragingly.

'Yeah, but um...,' she hesitated. 'I'm not sure if the door is securely latched,' she pointed her finger toward the door.

I returned to her room a minute later affirming its locked position. We began kissing and this time it was the curtains that bothered her. Exasperated, I got up and drew them.

'What if...'

But she didn't complete whatever nonsense she was coming up with this time as I inserted my tongue deep in her mouth.

I brought my hands close to the bottom of her *kurta,* pulled it upward, and thankfully this time she raised her arms in anticipation without a fuss. She then helped me with my shirt. I fumbled behind her back with the strap of her bra and she couldn't resist her fit of giggles. With a wry smile she helped me with it. When it was undone, she coyly brought her arms close to her chest. I lifted her and settled her in my lap, then leaned backward resting my back on the bed. She was over me and we kissed passionately. I rolled my tongue over her ears and then glided it down at a snail's pace to the back of her neck as she oohed and aahed. I slowly glided it down further to the front of her neck and further down.

I realized something was wrong as I still wasn't stiff. I darted my eyes around and it definitely had to be the femininity of the room. We got up and I asked her to take us to Priyank's room.

This time around I was tugging at her hand and she guided me from behind to my great batch mate's room. I was aghast and stunned to find it the exact replica of her room. My mouth formed a perfect 'O' and it stayed that way for a full minute. Or was it two?

'What the hell are teddies and soft toys doing in a guy's room?'

'He loves them,' she replied, covering her breasts with her arms.

'And the pink colour all over?'

'Pink is his favourite colour as well,' she grinned in pride. 'We have very similar likes and dislikes,' she declared, nodding as though it were the most normal thing in the world.

Oh God, kill me!

I shook my head and made a mental note in my head to laugh over it later with Joe Singh.

We entered his room and I made her lie on his bed first and then clambered over her. We continued kissing and slowly I inched below to her neck, breasts, and belly running my tongue playfully, and then upward, and then down again. I unbuttoned her jeans and slowly pulled it down exposing her beautiful legs. I lifted her buttocks to remove her panty which was - anybody's guess - a pink colour with...*cute little bunnies all over it...*

Wait a minute...Oh my God! That was exactly the same panty that Priyank wore which we'd removed to apply tooth paste in his...bum. Oh Lord, so they wear...identical panties?

I made another mental note to tell this to Joe Singh later.

'What happened, what are you thinking?' Aisha asked, breaking my repugnant thought.

'Nothing,' I shrugged.

I let the thought pass and removed my clothes. Lying down beside her I took her in my arms. Our naked bodies entwined against each other and...we thought we heard something.

A doorbell!

'Oh my God! Oh my God!' she screamed in horror. 'Who's it this time, did I not tell you somebody might come.' She leaped on the floor and hastily collected her clothes.

I tried to calm her and tiptoed toward the door. When I peeped through the tiny glass hole I was struck with revulsion.

It was Priyank Bhatia! Perfect timing, asshole!

I trotted back inside nervously and informed Aisha. She managed to muffle her scream covering her mouth with her hands. We wore our clothes hurriedly and proceeded to the drawing room. I sat on the couch pretending to have a normal conversation.

'Hey, look who's here,' Aisha greeted her brother histrionically as she opened the door. 'Guess who's come to meet you brother?'

'Who? And why did you take so long to open the door?' Priyank asked suspiciously as he entered.

'It's your batch mate Ronit!' she announced, ignoring his second question.

Priyank turned round and I'll never forget that look of horror on his face. 'What the hell are you doing here?' he screamed.

I narrowed my eyes at Aisha. 'Thanks for having me over Aisha.' I got up and started for the door.

'Oh brother, he came to meet you, said he was in the neighbourhood, so thought of checking on his old batch mate,' Aisha said, cocking her head toward me.

He'll never buy this shit!

'I don't believe you sister.' He shook his head and widened his eyes at me. 'He'll never come and meet me...something is wrong.' He paused. 'You remember I used to tell you sister about some guys in my institute who bullied me all the time...' He trailed off, battling the lone tear in his eyes.

No, please don't, please don't say it. I looked at Aisha who watched her brother in despair.

'It was him!' he said, pointing a baleful finger at me, 'and one of his friends Joe.' His throat tightened and his voice was hollow. 'They used to tease me so much and...um...you know, the toothpaste thing I told you about...' He struggled to speak and tears abound found their way out his eyes.

'It was *them*! And then another time they splashed my underwear with itching powder. You know the entire day they laughed watching me scratch my...my balls. They even told... um...wait a minute...' He paused and suddenly went silent. He glanced at me and Aisha back and forth a couple of times and then raised his eyebrows in shock and looked toward Aisha again.

'OH MY GOD!' he hollered as something hit him. 'Is *he* the guy you have been dating you told me about...' Amidst the tears, he was fuming now, '...and *oh my God! Have you guys been having sex?*'

He plunked down dejectedly on the sofa, and sobbed profusely with long, heaving motions of his chest. 'Oh my God, my own sister is...sleeping with...with...my *enemy!*'

I looked apologetically at Aisha who already had a look of hatred in her eyes. This was pretty much the reason I'd always managed to convince her not to tell about us to him. 'Let the right time come, we'll tell him then,' I used to tell her.

She joined her brother, sat beside him on the couch, and gently rubbed his back. 'Sorry brother, I had no idea that was him.' She looked at me with bloodshot eyes. 'You guys put toothpaste in his butt? Shameful!' she said.

I tried very hard to stifle a laugh. Now that *did* sound funny. What sort of a brother would tell that to his sister?

Although I should have felt sorry for the scene unfolding in front of my eyes, but somehow, I managed to amuse myself by laughing within. I *have* to tell all this to Joe Singh. I made another mental note. *Phew! How many notes have I made already?*

Alright, time to clean the mess I made.

I walked over to Priyank and sat on the floor on my knees resting my arms on his laps. A few tear drops of his fell on my arms. 'Look brother, I am sorry, very sorry for what I did three years back. We were kids back then and just having a good time. We didn't mean to hurt you, and if at all we did, I'm really sorry from the bottom of my heart.

'But I love your sister. I really love her, and howsoever she pretends to hate me because of what I did to you, she knows deep down she loves me too. So please forget what happened in the past and let's make a fresh beginning.' I paused for a brief moment to let it all sink in. I looked at Aisha and then at Priyank. I don't know if that convinced him but at least it managed to assuage the intensity of his wails. 'Okay brother, I'll do anything you tell me to for repentance, just give me one chance.'

His head shot up the moment I said that, and he eyed me ominously. 'Anything?'

'Anything,' I confirmed, pressing his hands.

Ten minutes later I was butt naked in his room on all fours as Priyank and Aisha squeezed their mint tooth paste inside me.

I made another mental note to remove all other mental notes in my head, and *not to tell anything* of this evening to Joe Singh.

10. THE MARRIAGE PROPOSAL
January 2011, Mumbai

Almost seven years in our relationship and I was still apprehensive of asking Aisha to marry me. I'd actually asked her innumerable times in so many years but it still made me sweat. I couldn't wait to spend the rest of my life with her and have her kids.

But she'd always told me she didn't want to get married, so soon, I mean. So after my first proposal in the first year of our relationship on that beautiful evening we spent on Marine Drive, I waited more than six years for her to grow older. And now, here we were, still confronting the same question.

Thankfully, Priyank didn't play a spoilsport and had been supportive of our relationship ever since I agreed to his whacky demand. He didn't leave it there, though. After I was back in my clothes, groaning with pain, he told me if I ever troubled his sister like I'd troubled him, he'll squeeze the toothpaste again.

It had been two more times since then.

Now, we were in Mumbai as my cousin was getting married. Since my family was here, it had to be the perfect time for the proposal. I'd thought of setting a meeting of my parents with Aisha's after she agreed.

After strolling through the busy streets of Bandra (she had to do some shopping, I was told), we chose a Chinese restaurant for lunch. As we entered, the scent of ginger and garlic was overpowering. It was dimly lit and hoops of yellow luminescence were cast by low-arched bulbs. The restaurant was moderately occupied, and we ran our eyes for a perfect place to sit. We chose the seats at the far end, and Aisha plunked down on the couch.

'Eh, perfect,' she muttered under her breath, looking around, surveying the restaurant.

'It is,' I agreed, settling on the chair across her. She would always choose the couch.

The waitress handed us the food and drinks menu and excused herself. I handed Aisha the food menu.

'Thanks,' she nodded, leafing through the menu, 'for bringing me to such a nice restaurant, I mean,' she said, darting her eyes all over the place.

'Any time, sweetie,' I winked at her.

'Wait a minute...' she said and placed the menu on the table and eyed me suspiciously. 'Have you called me here to propose?'

I cringed. 'Yes,' I gulped the sparkling water.

'Oh Ronit!' she waved her hands dismissively and crashed back in her seat. 'How many times have I told you I don't want to get married so soon? I'm just twenty-three,' she protested. 'And you are what...twenty-four?'

'Twenty-five, actually.' I corrected her.

'See!' she squinched up her nose. 'We are still so young. There'll be so many fights after our marriage.'

'No baby,' I said in a soft whisper, 'it's us you are talking about. We'll *never* have a fight. I just can't wait to get married to you.'

She didn't look at me and neither did she respond.

'Aisha, look,' I said, feeling the blood rush to my cheeks. 'I love you so much and can't live without you. I don't care if we are young; I just want to be around you all the time. I want to wake up next to you, have kids with you. I want you to be the first and last person I see every day. I want to hold you in my arms all day long and not wait for your parent's permission so that you could meet me.' I took a deep breath before resuming. 'I can't be taking flights to Mumbai every now and then just so I can see your lovely face. I miss you so much when I'm in Delhi. My life is perfect with you in it; you have brought out the best in me. Besides, it's been seven years already, we don't need any more time to be sure of each other.'

'Aw,' she said, 'that was so sweet.' She smiled, reached out for my hand, and squeezed it. 'Alright then, Ronit, let's do this.'

'Really?'

She nodded. I breathed a sigh of relief and thanked my stars. Finally I would marry the love of my life.

Over food, we discussed about our parent's meeting. Finally, I could see that elusive excitement over her face. Yes, we were getting married. Life couldn't have been better. I decided to tell Joe Singh.

No! He always gave me the wrong advice.

I couldn't believe it. Our parents refused.

No, not for the marriage (thankfully), but not so soon! According to Aisha's parents, Priyank should get married first because she, I mean he, was the elder one.

'We also have an elder son,' Aisha's mother stroked her hand affectionately over Priyank's hair, 'and we want to get him married before Aisha. I hope you understand Mrs. Kapoor,' she said to my mother earlier this afternoon.

'Of course,' my mother had replied. 'We ourselves are not keen of it so soon. Rohit is just twenty-four.'

'Twenty-five!' I'd said through clenched teeth.

The same evening I was pacing nervously in my room. I wasn't going to give up so easily and decided to convince first my parents and then Aisha's parents. I wanted to marry her as soon as possible. For a fleeting moment, her mother's words played in my mind. *We also have an elder son and we want to get him married first before Aisha.* Seriously now I had to wait for *Priyank* to get married? Will that even happen in the first place? It would have been easier to look for a man to get married to him, I wanted to tell her.

Shunning the thoughts, I sauntered to my mother's room pondering over the various options in my head to break the ice with her. My mother was the quintessential doting Indian mother whose life revolved around her children. It wouldn't be too difficult to convince her.

'Mom, I want to get married to Aisha at the earliest,' I gurgled out, feeling queasy in my stomach.

She removed her glasses, set aside the magazine she was reading, and leaned forward. 'What's the hurry, Pinkoo?'

Outlandish yes, but that was my pet name. So now you know why I hate the colour pink.

'Because I have waited for her for seven years and because-'

She agreed. She had to; no mother could see tears in the eyes of her child, howsoever fake. But only one condition she had told me - our *kundlis* or whatever they are called should match.

They didn't. Another bucket load of tears! She agreed. But one final condition – there should be an auspicious date.

There wasn't. Not until the next six months, I mean, and I wasn't going to wait for Aisha for that long. And yet again I cried. Seriously was I becoming Priyank now?

However, this time my mother didn't agree. She said it would be a bad omen without the *kundlis* and suitable date. I told her if not within the next month, I will *never* get married. Her heart melted and she agreed. So that was one target out of the way!

Next in line were Aisha's parents. Aisha had told me that her parents were very adamant about getting Priyank married first, they would never agree. So I asked Aisha to set a meeting with her, I mean him.

We sat in a café near their house, and ordered three cappuccinos. Priyank ordered a couple of cookies.

Slowly sipping my coffee, I fidgeted in my seat, and looked coyly at Priyank wondering how to even start. Aisha had not told him about the objective of the meeting at my behest. She bit her lip nervously rolling her eyes.

'So Priyank,' I began casually, 'when do you plan to tie the knot?'

He blushed. Seriously.

'I don't know...' he said and scratched his eyebrows awkwardly, '...may be when I find a nice and homely girl.'

Homely girl? 'Okay, that's nice to hear,' I replied. 'Priyank um…I was just wondering,' I cleared my throat and Aisha looked elsewhere pretending not to be a part of the conversation, 'if you could please tell your parents that you don't want to get married for the next um…five years, may be till you become a Captain.'

Priyank eyed me sceptically. He gave me one of those hmm-I-know-what-you-are-thinking looks. 'And why would I do that?'

'Don't you love your sister?' I asked him dramatically. Aisha snooped in with an innocent look on her face. 'She's dying to get married soon but with you in the way…um…you know, she can't,' I ended.

Priyank looked at his sister in anger. 'You want me to get married five years later?' he asked with a look of disbelief.

'Oh no, no brother, not at all…' she said and held up her hands defensively, 'you didn't understand. What Ronit is trying to say is that you tell this to mother so that *we* can get married soon. You know she wouldn't tell me to wait for five years then. And after our marriage you can do it whenever you want, no problem,' she conceded, looking at me confused.

'Oh my God! I'm the elder one and you want to get married *before* me.'

I remembered our institute days. Bugger *had* to come first at everything after all. We proffered him an understanding nod and waited for him to calm down.

'Please brother, for us, please,' Aisha pleaded.

'Please brother, please, please,' I begged, folding my hands.

He gritted his teeth and violently shook his head. 'Never!'

'Please brother, please, I'll do anything for you.' I found myself saying that again and regretted it a moment later. Last time those words had proved to be quite expensive.

'Anything?' His eyes shot up and he asked me in that familiar ominous gaze.

I took a moment to answer. 'Anything brother,' I finally said.

A minute later I called up Joe Singh and requested him for something. After forty-five minutes of requesting, pleading, begging, he finally agreed.

'Dude you owe me big time for this one,' he yelled before snapping the phone.

The next day I took Priyank over to Joe Singh's place when he was alone.

Priyank had mint tooth paste in his hands.

And so I managed convincing everybody. Almost a month later, on 14 February 2011, we got married. I was the happiest man in the world.

11. A MONTH IN CAPTIVITY
July 2011, Somewhere in Somalia

Happiest man, my foot!

Well, if you want to know how to dig your own grave, you know whom to ask.

I can't believe that I actually convinced everybody for my marriage The question has been ringing in my head again and again, and I can't believe I actually did that. No one wanted us to get married so soon, not even Aisha. I should have at least enjoyed a few more years of my bachelorhood, and then, who knows the relationship might have fizzled out on its own. That has to be the biggest irony of my life.

My wife is partly the reason I am stuck with these pirates today. The amount of anger and frustration I had amassed just a few months after our marriage made me leave my house in a fit of rage. I remember so many times I was told by my company that this ship transits Somalia and they would give me a better option a month later. The crew manager of the company is my maternal uncle - hence the consideration - but I didn't pay any heed. I just wanted to be away from my wife for a while, anywhere, even in hell. And well, here I am, actually in hell.

It's been a month now and we are still awaiting the response from our company. All of us have been kept huddled on the bridge with very limited access to food and water. Although we do get food but it's only once every day in the form of steamed rice. Sometimes we get boiled potatoes along with it and rarely a vegetable which is anyway inedible. But there's no fixed timing of when the food would arrive and that's what makes it all the more excruciating. Other than that we get only half a bottle of water every day which is muddy brown in colour. We use a cloth to filter it as there's no other choice to quench our thirst. We are not even allowed to move here without their permission. They let us call home just once last week to ask our families to put pressure on the company for the ransom. I had called my mother and cried on the phone with her. The thought of calling Aisha didn't even occur to me.

Fortunately they haven't killed or hurt anymore of us after our cook. However, we live under constant mental strain with death threats if they don't get their ransom.

Over the last few days we have noticed a slight change in their behavior toward us. They appear more impatient and agitated as the company hasn't agreed to their demands yet. They constantly drink in front of us but thankfully, at most, yell or abuse us.

'Hey you, motherfucker!' my thoughts are interrupted by the growl of one of them. Abuses have become a regular affair nowadays. All of us turn toward the surly voice.

'Who are you staring at, bastard?' One of the pirate barks at our third engineer. 'Eyes down, motherfucker!' the pirate gets up in an alcoholic haze and walks toward him. 'Eyes down, I said.'

The third engineer panics and roots his eyes to the ground. From the distance I can see his hands trembling.

'Stand up, stand up bastard!'

The third engineer looks around in fear. Beads of sweat form on his forehead and he runs a shaking hand across his face to wipe it. His body shudders and he struggles to rise on his feet. 'S-s-sorry…sir.'

'Who were you staring at bastard?' The pirate launches himself at him and punches the third engineer in his face, once, twice…repeatedly. There is a crunching sound of a bone and the third engineer whines with pain. 'S-sorry sir, p-p-please stop…'

His whining enrages the pirate further and he punches him again and again, unleashing his fury at him. He swings his arms wildly and smashes his fist on the third engineer's already broken nose and jaw alternately. His other companions continue with their drinks, laugh, and encourage him.

All of us freeze in fear but we know we can do nothing to stop him. Blood oozes out from the third engineer's face, and the pirate breaks some of his teeth before throwing him back on the floor. 'You fucker, don't you dare stare at me again!'

The third engineer groans with pain covering his face with his hand. Blood spurts out from between his fingers. He squirms on the ground sobbing, screaming, begging…for help. My lips tremble at his agonizing sight and I resist the urge to offer him first aid.

The second officer thinks the better of it and scampers across the bridge over the medical drawer.

'Hey you, asshole!' the pirate screams at the second officer. 'What the fuck! Where are you going?'

'I'll…give him some…medical help.'

'Come here you bastard,' the pirate bellows. 'Come, come here!' He hurls his arms out at him.

Warily, the second officer trudges toward him, and sneaks a frightening glance at me and Captain. I draw out my hands helplessly and silently admonish him. Just then the pirate takes a big step forward and swings his arms violently across his face.

'Bastard, who do you ask before you move, huh?' He hollers and slaps the second officer repeatedly. 'Who you ask?' he shouts again, and when he doesn't get the answer, flings his arms continuously at the second officer. He says something in their language to one of his companions who nods and sprints outside to follow his orders.

The pirate keeps thrashing the second officer interspersing the hitting with his question, 'Why you no ask somebody, you motherfucker, huh, why you don't take permission?'

His companion returns a minute later with a canister of... OIL.

Oh my God! What is he planning to do?

I shoot a frightening look at Captain. The horror in his eyes is mirrored in my own. When I glance back at them my worst fear turns into a dreadful reality when the pirate splashes oil all over the second officer's body. I glance at Captain again who waggles his finger signalling me not to act.

I know that Captain but they are...

But I know Captain is right. There is no way we can stop whatever these guys have thought.

'P-p-lease sir, s-s-sorry sir, p-p-lease don't do this, p-please...' The second officer shivers in trepidation and begs the pirate who stands in front of him sneering with a match stick in his hand.

'Ha, ha, ha, bastard,' the pirate laughs, looking at his companions and the second officer back and forth. All of them laugh and support him. 'You fuck with us, we'll fuck you!'

'S-s-sorry sir, very, very s-s-sorry,' the second officer pleads again.

All of us watch in horror. I feel like a spineless, impotent man who can do nothing to help my fellow mate. My heart throbs loud against my chest and my breathing has grown fast and shallow. I do a silent prayer in my head. *Please God, help him, please, please.*

And just then the unthinkable happens...There is a collective loud gasp when the pirate flicks the match stick in direction of the second officer. Seconds later his whole body is in flames.

'Oh God!' I whisper to myself, my hands clasped against my mouth.

Amidst the flames, the second officer is screaming and wincing. He cavorts all over the bridge, and searches helplessly for a cloth or water to smother the fire.

The pirates continue laughing and smirking. 'Look at him now, ha, ha,' one of them says.

'H-h-h-help me someone, p-p-lease, please...,' he keeps yelling amidst the flames but we do nothing. Some of us cry and others have pressed their eyes shut with their hands clasped to their ears. I keep glancing at the pirates hoping they would stop this madness soon. But they don't.

Instead, a few minutes later, one of them pokes a driftwood in second officer's chest and guides him outside the bridge, moving ahead with him, toward the railings, and with a little help of his hands pushes him in the water.

'Captain!' The pirate who initiated the fire bellows and makes his way over to the side toward the Captain. 'Tell your people to behave and follow our orders. You understand!' He glares at Captain who nods slowly. 'And why we still not receive any money, huh? Why? Already one month now. Call your company and tell them we will kill you all one by one if we don't get our money. OK! You understand that? Go, call now!'

Captain gets up hurriedly and rushes toward the satellite phone for the call. I'm not sure if that can help us now.

I swallow hard and the memory of *that afternoon before the pirates boarded* flashes in my mind. I was sitting with the Captain in his room nattering about our love stories and marriage. *It all started from there...* All those questions about his incomplete love story for which I yet don't have the answers emerged that afternoon.

Only if we had been a little more careful that day...all this wouldn't have happened in the first place. The pirates wouldn't have boarded and the second officer wouldn't have been...

The screams of the second officer ring loud in my ears, and those ghastly images frame my mind.

I'm sure now; sooner or later we'll all end up that way.

PART ~ 2

12. THAT AFTERNOON BEFORE THE PIRATES BOARDED - 1
25th June 2011, Transiting Indian Ocean

It had been close to two weeks since I joined this ship. I had never been so delighted to leave my country and my home. Why not? I was getting complete freedom from Aisha for three months.

However, I did feel lonely now and then, and something inside me had died. After all I had loved Aisha for seven long years.

That made my stay here quite the opposite of what I'd expected. Sure, I was free to do whatever I wanted, whenever I wanted; nobody told me not to put the wet towel on the bed, to put my socks in my shoes and not throw them just about anywhere, to hang my jeans and shirts on the hooks and so on, but I felt something tugging at my heart strings.

Nevertheless, I'd made up my mind to divorce her the moment I set my foot back in India, and never to get married again. The pain and disappointment this marriage has inflicted upon me is certainly not worth the effort I had to make. Why did I not listen to Joe Singh? He'd warned me so many times. And now, I'll have to bear the repercussions of it for the rest of my life. I haven't even thought of how much alimony I'll have to pay her, by the way.

I'd been dawdling my time here not a tad interested in any work. I don't speak to anyone, and my conversations with my fellow crew members are restricted to the incumbent hellos in the mess room. Whenever I find time, I plop down on my bed and try to catch some sleep. When I am awake I daydream.

But I'll be okay once I get past the initial hangover, I'd been telling myself. After all, I'd seen the worst in my relationship.

Quite a few times I thought the Captain could sense there is something wrong with me, by the way he looks at me through the corner of his eyes while we are seated in the mess room. He's quite observant I believe. Either that or he is good at reading faces. He'd asked me a couple of times 'Are you okay?' I'd shrug and wave my hand dismissively. 'Of course,' I'd tell him.

Then today in the afternoon over lunch he asked me over to his cabin for a drink. Although not in the mood of mingling with anybody, I couldn't say no to the drink.

An hour later, I knocked on his door gently and decided that I would just have one drink, and leave early without talking much.

He opened the door and had a pleasant smile on his face as he welcomed me in his cabin. I could see his brown eyes twinkle behind his glasses. He led me toward the couch and we settled on it sitting across each other.

'So Ronit, how's your stay turning out to be?' he asked casually, settling back in his seat.

'So far, so good sir,' I replied. *Okay, where's the drink?*

He nodded and stared intensely at me through his stony eyes from above the rim of his glasses. I cringed in my seat and avoided his gaze by looking around.

'Oh, what's that?' I tried distracting him, pointing toward an old worn out diary on the table.

He picked the diary and ran his fingers poignantly through it. 'That's my personal diary,' he replied wistfully.

'It looks pretty old,' I said quickly. It was in tatters, worn out from the edges, and had to be a dozen years old at least. 'Why can't you get a new one, we have plenty of them in the store.'

'Oh no,' he sighed. 'I don't want a new one.'

I nodded.

'Oh sorry, I almost forgot,' he said, keeping his diary aside. 'What will you have, beer or whiskey?'

'Whiskey, sir.' *Yes, I needed that.*

'Right away.'

He rose to his feet and started for his living room lifting the two glasses from the table. I planned to leave after the first drink feigning a headache or something.

'Soda or water?' I heard his loud voice from inside his living room.

'Soda sir,' I called out, straightening up on my seat.

He returned a minute later with two glasses filled with golden liquid. We clank our glasses and drank in silence when he surprised me with his abrupt question.

'So Ronit, what is bothering you?' he asked, lowering his head.

I don't like anyone probing in my life, especially a stranger. How much do I know him anyway? 'Nothing sir,' I replied, shrugging.

'Look son,' he continued, leaning forward and placing his glass on the table, 'my hair didn't become gray in the sun. I've been a Captain for more than twenty years, seen the entire world, worked with a lot of nationalities. I know exactly when something is wrong with someone.'

'I understand sir, but really nothing is wrong,' I pressed.

'Alright,' he said.

He picked up his glass, took a sip, and settled back in his seat.

'You know,' he continued slowly. 'I lost my wife when I was somewhat your age, I mean in a divorce,' he clarified instantly. 'But even today when I feel depressed about it, I talk it out. It makes me feel better.'

I smiled weakly. 'Actually even...um...my wife and I plan to get a divorce this time.'

'Oh,' he sighed, 'I am sorry to hear that.'

'No,' I dismissed, 'it's alright. I want to be done away with it anyway.'

'So, what was it, arranged marriage?'

'No,' I shook my head. 'Actually love marriage.'

'Oh...and how long have you guys been...married?'

'I've known her for the past seven years, but um...' I felt a knot tighten in my stomach. '...we've been married for just four months.'

'Really!' He raised his eyebrows. 'And you guys plan to get a...divorce. Don't you think these are still early days in your marriage?'

'Yeah, I know...' I looked down at the floor before facing him. 'I know sir but...I think that's the best for both of us. She is a bitch really, can't stay with her anymore.'

'Ha, ha!' he laughed. 'That's what I used to think of my wife before the divorce.'

I looked up to face him. 'Really, so why did *you* guys get a divorce?'

'Ah,' he shrugged, 'that was a long time ago. You won't be interested, it's a long story.'

'You can tell me sir; maybe I can learn something from it.' I found myself opening to him now.

'If you really want to learn from my mistakes, all I can advise you is never, ever turn your back on love.' He removed his glasses and leaned forward. 'Never do that, *never*. Have faith in the person you love and always be patient. Love has to be patient after all.'

I smiled. 'So what's your story, sir?' His words piqued my curiosity.

'You really want to know my story?' he asked squeezing the bridge of his nose.

I offered a nod.

'You know,' his voice was a whisper. 'It'll make you smile initially, but later, you'll cry.'

'Okay sir, go for it then, I'm all ears.' I was really drawn forward to this conversation and didn't realize was almost at the edge of my seat.

'Wait a minute!' He threw up his hands at me. 'You haven't told me anything about *your* story...'

'Okay.'

For the next fifteen minutes, I told him everything about Aisha: the day we first met at our graduation day, my first date with her, our first kiss, about her brother, and the way I convinced everyone for the marriage. We found ourselves laughing when I completed my story.

'You guys,' he stroked his finger at me affectionately. 'That sounds like a funny story to me. Where's the tragic part?'

'Oh,' I sighed, 'It's gonna come sir, it's gonna come. Let the marriage begin and you'll know.'

He caught my gaze and smiled. When he asked me for the second drink, I didn't refuse. Surprising myself I felt comfortable in his presence now. When he returned, I looked at him intensely. It was his cue to begin. He placed his glass on the table and settled back in his seat.

'Um.....let's see, so where do I begin?'

13. CAPTAIN'S STORY - 1
September 1969, Nagpur

I was eight years old when I first met Shikha. I still remember that day vividly. It was raining heavily and Baba had come back early. He was accompanied by his old friend Mahesh and his daughter, Shikha. Baba was meeting him after five years and both the friends were very excited. Shikha was wearing a white frock with some floral design on it and a red border. Her hair was tied neatly in two pony tails on either side and little strands of hair lined her forehead. Her eyes were big and wide, flushed with innocence, and a shade of fear. A year younger to me, she was all of seven then. I took her into my room, gave her some of my toys, and together we played for hours.

My mother had died at my birth but Baba never felt the need to get married again. He'd toil hard, had an unrelenting spirit, and made sure I wasn't denied of any worldly pleasures. My Baba was both my father and mother. His life revolved around me and my proper upbringing was his sole aim. We didn't have any other relatives, but with so much love and support I never felt the need. We were poor but had a decent roof over our head and everything else in between.

Mahesh uncle's wife had also died three years ago, battling cancer, so one day Baba asked him to move in with us.

'We won't have to pay rent for two separate flats so why

don't we live together, we'll have good company and the kids would get someone to play with.'

Mahesh uncle refused initially but with Baba's constant importuning, he finally gave in. I was very happy as I was getting a permanent friend in the house.

In the mornings both friends after serving us breakfast and dropping us to the nearby government school went to their respective offices and returned late in the evening. Since I was the elder one I was told to take care of Shikha. In the afternoon we'd saunter back to our flat, school bags slung over our shoulders and held each other's tiny hands. Baba would give us some money and on the way back, we had ice cream daily. Shikha was very fond of it; I'd just give her company. After the ice cream we'd hop and skip and jump our way back to our house. It was time for the toys.

Over dinner both Baba and Mahesh uncle had long conversations about politics, current affairs, business, and about their own lives. They enjoyed each other's company just like me and Shikha. They often laughed over the fact that they were happy as they didn't have a wife to pester them.

'No woman, no trouble,' Mahesh uncle would remark facetiously.

Baba would only smile back. But I was sure he never smiled from within. If he did, he would never slide the drawer open in his cupboard every night to look woefully at my mother's picture with tearful eyes, running his fingers on her face before he went to sleep. I loved Baba for that, he never got married again. I learnt the lesson of true and everlasting love from him.

Baba always emphasized the power of knowledge and education. He exhorted me to study hard and become wise; to get a good, respectable job, and earn enough money. He never wanted me to become a labourer like him. I promised I would make him proud some day.

Life went on. We had a good time those days – oodles of laughter of playing and running under the sun, having long juvenile chats, singing old Hindi songs, and the like. Soon, Shikha and I became best friends. We'd fight regularly though, but they seldom lasted for more than a few hours. We became so used to each other's company that being angry with each other was unnatural, as if that emotion never existed. With her around I never felt the need for any other friend. In fact, we never even had any other friends. Not by chance, but I guess by choice.

A few months later, one day over breakfast as they were talking about business, something hit them. They were both working as labourers in a textile mill and thought of starting their own venture. They knew they had the brains, right attitude, and both were hard working and driven. Moreover after working in the same industry they had a fair amount of an idea of how it worked.

Over the next few days, they did their research while working in their respective companies. They would toil late into the night analyzing and organizing their thoughts. They had very little savings which they would have to put at risk if they were to start a business. That got them thinking. Eventually they decided in favour of it and one day I saw Baba transferring his clothes from the cupboard to an empty suitcase.

'Are you going somewhere Baba?' I asked him hurriedly. I was playing with Shikha outside and had come in to grab a bottle of water as she was thirsty.

Baba smiled and stopped packing. He beckoned me toward him and sat me on his lap.

'Yes, we are going to Bombay for a few days to meet some people.'

I flinched. 'But Baba, why? How will I live without you?' I felt the warmth of tears on my face. I'd never been away from him.

Baba gave me a reassuring smile. 'It's only a few days, it's not as if we are going forever, and then when we are back, we'll start our own business. We'll have more money, a better house, and I'll send you and Shikha to a better school. We'll have a much better life Shekhar.'

I nodded meekly. 'But why can't we come with you if it's only for a few days.'

'No,' he said quickly, 'I don't want to you to miss your studies.'

I made a face. 'But Baba, why do you want to do business, we have a decent life,' I asked, my mind wandering outside. *Shikha would be waiting for me, she was thirsty.*

'Oh Shekhar, you are too young to understand this. Now go and call Shikha, Mahesh wants to speak to her.'

I heard Shikha's wails in the next room, the moment she tottered inside excitedly. She thought she'd be getting a chocolate.

'Okay Baba, but please be back soon, we don't know anybody else here.' I begged him when I returned to my room. Baba had finished his packing and was holding his suitcase in his hands. He gave me a reassuring wink.

An hour later, both were at the door with their bags giving us their final assurances and advice. Just before leaving, Mahesh uncle bent down on his knees and held my shoulders firmly looking me in the eye.

'You are a brave boy Shekhar, promise me you'll take good care of my daughter and never let her cry.'

'Of course, Mahesh uncle, I'll take care of her.' I gave him my word.

He kissed me and Shikha on our forehead and then they were gone. Shikha hugged me tight and tears trickled down her eyes. Suddenly I was the only one she had, at least for the next few days. I wiped my tears first and then Shikha's. Slowly we made our way back in the empty house. We hoped they would return soon.

They never returned. Two weeks later we got the news that their bus had met with an accident, killing all the passengers and they never even reached Bombay. The owner of our house threw us out as we didn't have any money to pay the rent.

With a heavy heart and tears in our eyes we stood alone and dejected on the road, the thought killing us that we had nowhere to go in this big, insolent world.

14. CAPTAIN'S STORY - 2
June 1970, Nagpur

It had been more than a month we'd been living on the footpath, without shelter and without much of food. Every morning I would trudge helplessly in the city in the hope of finding some work which would get me money to buy some food. Sometimes I got work - selling newspapers, cleaning garbage on roads, cleaning toilets – and sometimes I didn't. When I did, I would excitedly scamper down the street or wherever I was working at the end of the day toward Shikha, feed her with whatever little I could but made sure that I got her some ice cream. Her face would brighten up with its sight, and for once, I could make her smile. That was enough to keep me motivated and to run for work the next day.

During those days quite often we cried, commemorating our happier moments. Life obviously had been unfair to us. We lost had our mothers at a very early stage in our life and just when we were finally settled and content, God had taken our fathers too. Daily we'd wipe each other's tears and together shared the piercing thought of our loneliness.

The dark and lonely footpath had become our home. We would lie cuddled together under the dark sky, staring into its expanse in fear, in agony, and in the hope that someday our lives would be better. Sometimes we got sleep and at other times it was a long and patient wait for the sun to cast its first rays of sunshine. If at all we did get sleep, we hated waking up to the realization what our lives had become.

Then one day while strolling past the roads dejectedly in search of some work, I heard a loud clatter of children toward my right. I walked in the direction of the noise and observed a pale red coloured dilapidated building in the middle of a small playground where well over a hundred children were playing. I looked above at the board on the rusty metallic gate. It read: 'Bal Vidya Anathalaya'. My eyes widened in delight and it was my first happiest moment in a long time.

That was to become our home for the next decade.

I sprinted back toward Shikha, packed whatever little belongings we had and, entered the orphanage. The children were still playing and some of them glanced at us cheerfully. We were led to the small office by the gardener who saw us trudging aimlessly around the campus.

The office was on the ground floor of the building. It looked nothing like an office save for the files that lay cluttered and dust-ridden on the shelves. The woman in the office appeared to be in her fifties. She was short and plump and had an air of gaiety around her. *Children here call me Alka Ma'am,* she said with a dimpled smile after asking our names. In my ten years of stay at the orphanage rarely did that smile desert her exuberant face. Later, I would realize she had lost both her sons, and to fill the gaping hole in her heart, she surrounded herself with kids.

She filled out a few forms for us, asked us a few questions, and then cried with us hearing about our fathers. She encouraged us by telling us similar stories about the other children in the orphanage. For once it felt good to know that there were children like us in the world who have experienced similar pain and misery. She welcomed us to the orphanage and then asked Mohandas – the gardener - to show us around the little campus.

Mohandas was an agile man somewhere in his early sixties. However he had the memory of a fish. Twice we had to remind him who we were and why were we here. Shikha couldn't control her fit of giggles at his short term memory loss. It felt good to see her laughing; that smile had eluded her lips for over a month.

He showed us two big rooms that were adjacent to each other: separate accommodation for boys and girls. Each room had over fifty triple bunk beds. They were not very clean, but after living on the streets for a month, we weren't too fastidious ourselves. There was a small cleaning area, a dining hall, and four small classrooms. In it was the perfect home. God had been kind to us. My faith in Him was reaffirmed that day.

He told us that there were eighty-five children here in all - orphans like us, who had seen the worst life had to offer very early in their lives. They lived, played, and studied here. This was their home and it was good to see an air of affability around the campus.

We had a very methodical schedule in the orphanage. At six o'clock sharp in the morning, an alarm rang calling us for the morning prayers. Seven was our breakfast time and then it was study time from eight to one. That was my favourite time of the day. Of course, I had never forgotten the promise I'd made to Baba.

After studies, we had our second prayer at one followed by lunch. The rest of the afternoon and evening was spent in the playground indulging in physical activities. We had dinner at seven followed by the last prayer of the day. At eight o'clock, another alarm bell rang compelling us to go to bed. And then, lights of the campus would go out.

During our initial days Shikha and I spent most of our time together. We had our meals together, sat next to each other in the class and played with each other in the evenings. But as the days progressed, we became friends with almost everyone in the orphanage. We were like a huge family living, playing and celebrating life together. Soon the haunting memories of our fathers and loneliness deserted us and, once again, we were gifted a new life.

We had about four permanent teachers and a few others on voluntary basis. Together they taught us English language, math, science, history, general knowledge and physical education.

There were many memorable incidents of those days that are embedded deep in my mind. On one such occasion our English teacher had asked us what we would want to be when we grew up. One by one we began replying. There were various replies – engineers, lawyers, teachers, sport persons, etc. When my turn came, I said I wanted to become a very rich man and open a lot of orphanages. All the children including the teacher burst out laughing. But the story isn't done; Shikha had an even better answer. When her turn came she stood up from her seat nervously, and looking at me, answered, 'I want to be Shekhar *bhaiya's* wife.'

I can still remember vividly the teacher falling off her seat before bursting in a fit of laughter.

Evenings were the best time of the day. We played many games together. But there was one game I grew increasingly fond of over the months – hide and seek.

We'd play it together with a few other children. Quite often Shikha would find herself 'out'. It was never by chance really, because when she would hide, she could never control herself from giggling when the seeker approached her, manifesting her presence. During her turn to find others, she'd walk behind a tree and count from one to hundred loudly. It would take her ages to complete it making us restless in our hidden position. And when finally she was ready for the hunt looking for us, she never managed to get herself out of it because she was so slow to respond. I'd sneak behind her furtively, reaching out for her with my arms and then gently tap her from behind. She'd turn around cautiously making me scream in exhilaration, '*Dhappa*', scaring her to the bones. I loved that look on her face. All others would emerge clapping and giggling and then she'd proceed, hopping her way to the back of the tree, counting again. I think she enjoyed that herself.

When not indulging in sports, we'd walk around the campus holding hands and conversed about how our day transpired. We'd always confide in each other, shared our stories, dreams and worries. Those days we had our own worries and concerns, by the way.

On one such instance, there was a niggling thought in Shikha's mind. A boy named Rajiv would tease her by calling her a cat because she wore her dark hair high in two ponytails on either side. He'd wriggle his arms and body toward her shouting, '*billi, billi...*' His other eight, nine year old friends would chime in and laugh contemptuously at her. Sobbing, she'd come to me narrating her harried tale. I promised her I'd do something about it. When they continued pulling her leg, I took it upon myself to teach them a lesson.

The following day we had a little fight in the mud and Rajiv ended up breaking two of my front teeth. I cried at the sight of blood and was immediately rendered first aid.

And that's when they began teasing me as well by calling me, '*bina daat ka budha!*'

Of course, we learned to ignore them then.

There were some days in our orphanage when we had a feast in our dining area. Some wealthy and noble people from the nearby area celebrated the birthdays of their children or their own anniversaries or such equally significant dates with us. The food would be on their account those days and our best food in months. Not that the food in our orphanage was bad or anything - I had deep respect for it, especially after struggling for it for over a month - but it had ceased to excite us. It was the same old rice and dal, with some dry vegetable, and desert on Sundays. We would rush through our meals to indulge in other interesting activities (like studying or playing hide and seek). Shikha would whine occasionally that there wasn't any ice cream here. So, to honour her demand, I requested Sheila aunty and Ramesh uncle – our regular visitors – to get us loads of ice cream on their next visit. They happily agreed to it and tousled my hair affectionately.

However, I got a rebuke that day from our teacher who told me I should be taught manners. But I couldn't care less. I had done that for Shikha, my sweet little Shikha, anything for her!

Since then whenever they'd arrive, Shikha would scamper to the entrance gate to have her share of ice cream. I wondered why she was so crazy about it. The thought of opening my own brand of ice cream someday for her often crossed my mind.

There was another wonderful thing I remember from those days. After our last prayer of the day, Shikha would make sure to wish me 'goodnight' with a tight hug every night before going to bed. It had almost become customary and on days she'd forget it, she'd dart to my room, would wake me up from my sleep (howsoever deep that might be), and then give me that hug.

I still cherish that sweet little gesture.

And so life went on. Days became months, months became years, and over time our fondness for each other deepened. It wasn't too long before I would discover the joy and magic of first love.

15. CAPTAIN'S STORY - 3
July 1975, Nagpur

I was all of fourteen when I first realized I was madly in love with Shikha. It wasn't a revelation that surprised me, part of me had known this was coming, but the inundating force with which it hit me took me by surprise.

The first rains of the season had arrived and Shikha had grown increasingly fond of it over the years. She'd love dancing under the rain with her face tilted toward the dark gray sky, eyes at rest, and savoured the moment as little drops of rain slammed across her face. All her sadness and worries evaporated with the heat in the air and she'd prance all over the muddy ground with few of her other friends. I'd hide behind a tree secretly admiring her simplicity.

Shikha had turned out to be a pretty girl - her comely features, high cheekbones, and full lips adding to her charm. She had big, wide, communicating eyes, and long hair cascaded down her shoulders. It was then that the thought of spending the rest of my life with her first occurred to me.

Though one would wonder, such thoughts of love were premature at that age, but then love doesn't have a manufacturing date. It doesn't have an expiry date either. It just happens like that making you feel overwhelmed. It does not wait for people to grow, it doesn't wait for the right time, it just happens.

And I'm glad it happened to me.

Those days I could sense an appreciable amount of change in the way I looked at her, the way it felt when I took her hands in mine, or the way we hugged before bed time. It was as if the man in me was awakening. A few missing heart beats here and there, that lingering smell and touch of hers in my hands, the picture of her pretty face that adorned by mind were the sort of stuff I never felt before. Things felt different... *and wonderful.*

Then one day the thought of conveying my feelings to her struck me. I had not planned on anything fancy though. I thought of taking permission from Mohandas to pluck a rose from the backyard but then decided against it. He would forget anyway.

After our lunch, when we had the entire evening to ourselves, I walked her over to the front ground. We sat on the green rusty bench and shared amicable glances. Although I had known her for six years, I must admit that I did feel the occasional knot forming in my stomach, that lump in the throat almost choking me, and surprisingly I was...nervous.

Come on it's just Shikha, I repeated in my head over and over again. But that didn't help.

Observing the hesitation in my demeanour, she eyed me askance, narrowing her eyes at me. She began tilting her head, rolling her eyes behind me and...she saw the rose. Instantaneously both her hands flew to her gaping mouth.

'Oh my God, Shekhar, you got a rose for me,' she finally said, resting her hands on the bench. 'That is so sweet, why are you hiding it?'

'Really,' I said, fidgeting in my seat and adjusted myself, 'that is…sweet.' I brought my hand forward that hid behind my back and handed her the rose.

'Of course,' she cackled, accepting the flower, and then brought it near her nose. 'It smells great.'

'Well…thanks,' I said. 'But…um…actually there's something else I wanted to talk to you about.'

She signalled with her eyes to continue, still immersed in the fragrance of the rose.

I tried to appear more confident than I actually was. I pulled up a strong face and girded myself.

'I think I'm falling in love with you,' I finally blurted out with clenched fists and my eyes half closed.

Shikha looked up from the rose and smiled coyly. Slowly she nodded before asking, 'You think?'

I considered her question and the instant revelation brought a smile to my face. 'No, not think; I'm sure I'm in love with you.' I was a lot more confident this time.

Shikha's eyes widened and her face tore open in a beatific smile. She clasped her mouth with both her hands again. I waited for a minute for her to speak. I thought she didn't realize I was waiting for an answer. Although I knew it in her expression, I wanted to hear those three words from her. Expression can't replace the significance of words.

'So, do…you?' I asked when I was sure there wasn't anything coming from her side.

'Of course,' she said. 'Of course, I love you Shekhar.' She held out her hands and placed them on my arms. I could feel the warmth of her touch. 'I don't want *anything* more in my life.'

I perked up on my seat. Sensing the easygoing air around us, I moved closer to her. She lifted her eyes to look into mine and then demurely looked away. I leaned forward toward her forehead with my eyes shut and kissed her softly. I retracted slowly and could almost hear her breath on my face. She wrapped her arms around me and I settled her face beneath my chin. We sat in that position for the next fifteen minutes until rain played spoilsport.

I can honestly say those had to be the best few minutes of my life until that point in time. I couldn't sleep the entire night.

Life felt more wonderful now. We suddenly got a new reason to live; our lives got a whole new meaning. Just sharing smiles across the room, eating food from the same plates, and hugging each other before bed time gave us such immeasurable happiness that only a person in love would understand. The nights went by dreaming about her and with the mornings came the joy and excitement of being with her, laughing with her, and looking into those two deep and beautiful eyes. Those had to be the best few months in our relationship which were to last another seven years before we got separated.

Meanwhile, life in the orphanage continued smoothly. We'd almost forgotten our pasts, and with so much love from our teachers and all other staff, it felt as if we'd been born here. We made some good friends along the way and some of them are my friends till date, especially Rajiv, the boy who broke my teeth a few years back.

He was a very fun loving and rebellious guy, I learnt later; somebody who would go down to any extent just to experience how a certain thing felt. On one such instance we had a nasty neighbour who often complained to our principal about the loud noise levels in the playground. We never reduced them anyway. One day just for the fun of it, to spite our neighbours, he smashed their window panes with pebbles. Later that day when asked by our principal the reason for that action, he simply replied that he wanted to see their reaction. Then one time he tied a bundle of crackers to their dog's tail. The poor dog twirled around the road in agony. There again he only wanted to experience the dog's reaction. I enjoyed his company; with him I learnt to live life spontaneously and without any restrictions.

Shikha had also made a couple of good friends whom she'd confide in. She was particularly fond of a girl named Swati. She was taller and slimmer than her and laughed easily. She had a story similar to ours and hence they bonded well. Shikha would tell me later about their girl talks and I'd have a good laugh.

With us, there was no such thing as privacy or our own space. We knew each other inside out. Our relationship was very transparent: if she did not like anything about me, she just told me; if I didn't like something about her, likewise. However in those years in the orphanage I guess that happened just once or twice. We just loved each other the way we were and believe it or not we never had any fight.

That is to say until we got married, of course.

Everyone in the orphanage had an inkling of our relationship when they saw us on the bench that day. And after that we made it very obvious. They were all very happy for us and the proverbial 'they are meant for each other' was on everyone's lips. Back then nobody had imagined us without each other. They knew we would spend the rest of our life together and encouraged us.

For orphans, finding a life partner meant the world to us. After spending most of our life in the chains of loneliness, that was the only way to break it. Any other place or school in those days, one would have looked down upon us. Instead of concentrating on our future we were in a relationship. One couldn't associate that with our age group. However here, it was the other way round. Everyone was encouraged to find their life partner in the orphanage itself, get married, and have a family. No wonder my relationship with Shikha was further bolstered. We never felt embarrassed walking with our hands together in front of our teachers and friends. Instead we got reassuring smiles.

However, I never let our relationship come in way of my studies. My teachers were proud of me and had faith that I'll do well in my life. I had to, for the plan. It was a simple one, though. All I wanted was to get a good job sometime later in my life, earn a lot of money so I could give Shikha a home and all the comforts of life she deserved, and then simply spend the rest of my life with her. It would take me some time to get there but I had a lot of faith in God. I knew he would be kind enough to me just as he had been in bringing us together.

But before that plan there was something else I had planned. There were a few boys in the orphanage who had part time jobs and after their studies left for work in the afternoon. I also wanted to get a job like them and earn some money. Although I never wanted anything for myself, the love for Shikha had always been more than enough for me, I wanted to buy gifts for her - clothes, ice cream, chocolates, and flowers - and pamper her. I wanted to take her out some days for movies and to good restaurants. I wanted to show my affection to her by doing all this and more. I wanted her to feel special, to feel she was the happiest and luckiest girl in the world. After all I had promised all that to her father the last time we saw him and Baba.

Promise me you'll take good care of my daughter and never let her cry...

Of course, I'll take care of her.

With that in mind, I wanted to be the perfect boyfriend and later the perfect husband any woman could ever desire. By the grace of god both my wishes got fulfilled.

Sadly, they didn't last long.

16. CAPTAIN'S STORY - 4
1979, Nagpur

How can someone be so much in love that everything in his life revolves around that person he loves? And why do these feelings never cease, instead flourish with each passing day?

I pondered over these questions as Shikha left the table for the washroom. We were sitting in a south Indian restaurant just a few blocks from our orphanage. It was a Friday and I had taken the day off so we had the entire day for ourselves.

Lately, we'd been indulging in a lot of extravagance - exploring restaurants, watching movies, sightseeing, and some shopping for Shikha. I had taken up a part time job for the last three years in a transportation company. For a few hours of service post noon, I was being paid reasonably well.

We'd been on quite a few dates in the past couple of years. Each time it was better than the last. I'd never speak in any of the dates much though. Actually, she never allowed me to. Having lived in the orphanage for almost a decade now, we knew the same people, had the same friends and we had nobody outside the four walls of the orphanage. Yet, she had the ability to generate an enormous amount of gossip. She went on yapping about her friends and I loved staring at her with a customary nod now and then, admiring her beauty.

She had turned seventeen a few months back and she was no more the cute little Shikha I had once known. She was easily the most beautiful woman I'd ever seen in my life. Apart from her charming looks, I always enjoyed her company; there was so much more to life when I was with her. Those days I had never seen her in a surly mood; even if she was, my presence would morph it to a congenial one. Our life was still akin to our relationship we had ten years back. Anger or coarseness never existed between us. It was as if we were the same person. I smiled at the thought that we were yet to have a fight.

'Hello there,' she clicked, breaking my thoughts. 'Where are you lost?'

I smiled looking at her. 'Where else?'

She smiled back. Yeah, she could read my mind.

I rose and reached out for her hands. We'd never walk without that; our fingers were always perfectly intertwined in each other's. I thought our hands were made for each other too. In the many years I'd known her, I must say that I have literally felt her hands grow in size. *When have I not been holding them?*

We'd watched the first day first show of the movie *'Shaan'* and we really liked it. It went on to become a super hit later. Shikha loved watching first day first shows, and well… I loved what she loved. So anticipating a mad rush at the ticket counter for an Amitabh Bachchan movie, I had scampered toward the cinema hall in the wee hours of the morning, and managed to get two tickets. I *had* to fulfil her little wish.

After the movie we had come for lunch here, although, I'd wanted to have lunch at a North Indian joint and she'd wanted fast food. So we'd settled for fast food initially. Then something hit her and she'd asked me casually, 'Why do we always do what *I* want to do?'

I smiled. 'Because both of us love you,' I'd said nudging her shoulders.

'But both of us love you too,' she'd replied instantly. 'So we'll have north Indian food today.'

'Shikha, that's not fair, you want to have fast food,' I'd protested.

'Yeah, but you want to have north Indian food,' she'd countered.

'But you don't *like* north Indian food, Shikha.'

'And you don't *like* fast food, Shekhar.'

And so we settled for a south Indian restaurant after five minutes of bickering.

After lunch we made our way to visit the geographical centre of India – the zero mile marker. Nagpur is precisely at the centre of India; hence this marker is located here. The distances of various major cities from here are carved on a pillar that is erected at this zero mile site. It was marked by the British and is located at the central part of Nagpur city. However the site didn't excite us much. There was hardly any prominent indication for locating the spot and the place although very significant, was mostly obscure. It was preserved in a small garden and we didn't even spend more than five minutes at the place.

After our boring visit to the zero mile marker both of us wanted to see something romantic and ethereal. And what could be better than lakes. Nagpur is home to many natural and manmade lakes. Sauntering on their banks, our hands together made for the perfect idea of a romantic walk. Whenever on a date, we made it a point to visit at least one of them. We'd seen most of them – Futula Lake, Telankadi Lake, Sakkardara Lake, Ambazari Lake, Gorewada and the Sonegaon Lake. Out of all of them, our favourite was the Futula Lake.

Mesmerizing sight, a good side walk, and a line of food joints at the foot of the lake often brought us here. It was a beautiful lake and a perfect destination to relax, enjoy and indulge in romantic conversations.

As we walked along its banks, Shikha rested her head on my shoulders. The entire world around me was out of focus and I was lost in her thoughts. We had made the decision of getting married a few years later when I get settled in my life with a good job. Shikha nudged me gently and nodded to a nearby bench. We made our way toward it.

It was a beautiful day, I observed, as I slipped my arms around her shoulders. Far away, the sun was an orange ball suspended in the sky. There were no clouds today making the sky appear a beautiful kaleidoscope of a hundred different colours. A gentle breeze carried the smell of wet sand. Together, we marvelled at the beauty that lay in front of us.

A smile emanated from her face. 'OK, baby, time for *dos* and *don'ts*.'

'OK.' I took a deep breath, retracted my hands, and looked ahead toward the beautiful lake. 'So I'll start with the *dos* first…'

In the last one year since the time we'd been discussing our marriage, she'd listed a few *dos* and *don'ts* for me. And almost every day she wanted to hear it so I never forget them.

'...I will always love you, respect you and care for you. I would say "I love you" innumerable times in a day. I would always surprise you and shower you with gifts. I'll always make you feel special and would always compliment you on your looks. On weekends, when at home, *I'll* cook and other days, I'll assist you with dinner when back from office. I would always kiss you and make love to you...'

'Ok, ok...' She brought her hands to her ears. 'Stop! Got it! Enough of the *dos*! Now the *don'ts*!'

'I'll never fight with you, will *never* argue, whatever you tell me will be the final verdict. I'll never abuse or hit you. I'll never even look at any other woman. I'll never do your bitching to anyone except you...' I trailed off, playfully cocking my head toward her.

'No, you won't even do that,' she warned me, wagging her finger.

'OK, I won't even do that. I'll never leave you and-'

'Never, ever!' she asserted, holding my arms tight.

'Yeah, never, ever,' I repeated. 'I'll never go to bed without resolving a fight that is to say if at all we have one...'

'Okay, Shekhar,' she interjected. 'That's enough; now remember each and every word of what you just said for the rest of your life.'

'I will,' I promised and we grazed our noses against each other.

Over the next few minutes, we were silent and appreciated the picturesque surrounding. We both knew there was still a lot of time before all that was to happen. We'd thought of getting married in our twenties, so there were still five years left. I needed that much time anyway to be somewhere in my life by then. But honestly, that felt too far. We wished if the next five years of our life vanished in a click and the next moment we were in each other's arms in our own house.

And yeah, we wished pigs could fly.

Our line of sight passed to a young couple and their two babies. Instantly, we looked at each other wistfully. We hankered for that life.

'So how many kids do you want Shekhar?' she suddenly asked, her eyes fixated at the family.

'At least five,' I replied without a thought.

'Yeah, me too,' she agreed. 'We should have a big family, something we never had. One child every two years, that would keep me busy for at least ten years straight. And maybe we can have more later if we still want to. Wow, that'll be so wonderful and then…'

She wasn't talking to me anymore, just mumbled words under her breath. I faintly nodded when something conjured up in my head. I turned my gaze toward her.

'Hey listen, why do we have to wait for so long to get married? Why can't we do it right away?'

Shikha frowned. 'I'm not even eighteen yet Shekhar, what are you saying?'

'Okay then, we'll get married when you turn eighteen, that's only few months away anyway.'

Her arms flew to her mouth. 'Really, we can do that,' she squealed in excitement.

'Of course! Why not? We'll just have to struggle initially but at least we can be together.' I looked in her eyes before resuming excitedly. 'So it's decided then, we'll get married the day you turn eighteen,' I declared.

Shikha only stared back at me in silence. And then, ever so slowly, little tear drops trickled down her eyes. I scooted closer and wiped them one by one. A little smile unleashed from her and I moved my face closer to hers. When she sensed what I was about to do, she hesitated initially, but then later closed her eyes and leaned forward.

And there, when our lips met for the first time, I knew it then, I would cherish this moment forever.

17. CAPTAIN'S STORY - 5
October 1980, Nagpur

It was a bright, sunny day with neither the crispness of winter nor the sweltering heat of summers.

The entire morning had been very exciting for all of us at the orphanage. It had taken a few hours for us to bid goodbye to each one of the wonderful people we'd grown with, in the last decade. All of them had tears in their eyes and best wishes on their lips. As we hugged each one of them, one moment we were crying, and the next instant a wide smile swept past our faces.

We were getting married today.

At nineteen and eighteen respectively, both Shikha and I were too young for marriage, we'd been told by all our elders in the orphanage. But then later, they thought, come on, it was us – the perfect candidates for marriage. It didn't matter if we were young or old. Absolutely nothing could have gone wrong in our case and we got their support eventually.

I had told Shikha after our marriage we'll move out of the orphanage and get a place of our own. I'd work during the day, she'd cook food for both of us, we'd make love at night, and well…lead a life like a normal couple does. She was hesitant initially but had later concurred with me. Staying in the orphanage after the marriage would take the fun of our new relationship. We knew it would be difficult for us to pay the rent while I go scouting for jobs, but then that didn't deter us. We had been through enough difficult times anyway.

So here we were, outside the district court of Nagpur, awaiting our witnesses – Alka ma'am, Rajiv and Shikha's best friend Swati.

Shikha was dressed in a sparkling red sari that wasn't too snazzy, with minimal make up, and her hair open on my insistence. We were holding hands outside facing each other awaiting our turn.

'You remember all your *dos* and *don'ts* Shekhar?' she grinned cheekily. 'Time to apply them.'

I gently lifted her chin with my forefinger. Her face dazzled in the warm sunshine and a gentle breeze blew past her hair. A lock of hair flew across her cheeks and I stretched my arms to tuck it behind her ears. I marvelled at the ethereal beauty in front of me that would be my wife in a few minutes from now.

'Each and every word of it,' I replied as I pulled her closer and she wrapped her arms around me. 'I love you so much,' I said.

'I love you too,' she replied and we pulled apart at the sight of our witnesses. We could see sweets and garlands in their hands.

Ten minutes later, our names were called and we hopped our way inside to the office.

And then, when we were back outside in the open, we knew our life would never be the same again.

I lifted her above my head and she spread out her arms, gazing at the sky above. She closed her eyes and her lips parted. I could sense she did a little prayer, perhaps, for a prosperous life ahead. I followed her gaze and when she looked down at me, her eyes were moist.

'Happy birthday, *wify*,' I said.

'Wow!' I exhaled a sharp breath. 'What a love story!'

'Hmm...,' Captain sighed, twirling his glass.

By his expression I was sure his mind was still in his story. His eyes were damp and he tried his best to avoid looking into mine. I felt my breath caught in my throat and I found it hard to speak. I wasn't sure anything I said would make a difference at this time anyway. His childhood sweetheart divorced him, and...three decades later he is still madly in love with her. I stayed silent and found myself overwhelmed by his grief.

'You want another drink?' he murmured. He still didn't meet my eyes.

'Sure sir.' I handed him my glass.

He rubbed his eyes with the back of his hand and sniffed loudly before getting up. While he was inside preparing drinks, I marvelled at the simplicity and innocence of his story.

'So...,' I cleared my throat, 'you were madly in love with her when you were just fourteen?' I asked him incredulously when he returned with the drinks. I could hear my voice shaking. 'Thanks,' I added when he handed over my glass.

He drew a deep breath. 'Yes, I was,' he replied and settled in his chair. A faint smile bordered his lips. He appeared slightly more composed now.

'In fact,' he added dreamily, 'I thought I was in love with her at the age of eight, barely few months after I first met her.'

'So then the million dollar question is why did you guys divorce, sir?' I said quickly. I had been struggling to find the answer to this question ever since he began narrating his story.

His face fell again and his expression grew solemn. He rolled his eyes sadly before turning them to me. 'Let's just say it was my mistake, I didn't understand her after our marriage.'

'You guys were one hell of a couple, come on, sir,' I replied in an animated expression. 'I mean you guys always thought about your partner before yourself. What was more to understand than that?'

'Yeah…I know…but…,' he trailed off and stared through the window toward the rippled gray water.

'So did you…um…file for divorce?'

'No, no,' he yelped, 'I would have never done that. She… she filed the divorce papers.'

'So, then sir, where is your fault?' I tried convincing him. I didn't like the glum expression on his face.

'Of course it is.' He thumped his fist on the table. 'It was my entire bloody fault.'

And it was then when I found myself crying along with him. It happened all of a sudden. One moment he appeared alright and the next moment he sobbed profusely, his shoulders shaking with the heaving motion of his chest. Never in my life had I seen a fifty year old man cry like that. And that made the situation all the more pitiful. I heard his pain-filled wails and it all turned out too much for me.

My stomach roiled and I cursed myself for asking him that question. It triggered all these emotions. I must have reminded him of...*something.*

'I'm sorry sir, so sorry.' It was all I could say.

He shook his head. 'I...I should have known the reason first.' He grunted through his tears. 'Instead my male ego took over and I threw the signed papers at her face and then slammed out of our house.' His words came out in broken gasps, filled with sorrow, anger...*guilt.*

I had nothing to offer other than a customary nod. Silence fell between us for a while and I couldn't believe the scene unfolding in front of my eyes. I came to his room for a single drink and had thought of leaving immediately after that. And here I was, patting his back, and was so drawn to his story that absolutely nothing else mattered. Surprisingly, I had even forgotten about my own story for a while.

He gathered himself together and his wails reduced to quiet whimpers. He wiped his tears and met my gaze.

'You know we were together for only six months after our marriage before we split, and I never even saw her face after that.' He shook his head in disbelief. 'Can you believe that? With so much love and affection, all it lasted was six months... only six bloody months?'

I nodded weakly, still struggling to come in terms with the reason. *Why? What happened?*

'I still love her so much; much more than I had ever loved her. I didn't marry again...actually, never even thought of it; her memories had always been enough for me. But all this wasn't until I realized that-'

The phone in his cabin rang. He reached for it.

'Good afternoon, Captain speaking.' He tried sounding normal. '...Okay...I see...how far...hmm...Okay, keep a watch on them. I'll be up shortly.'

I faintly listened to his conversation but my mind actually wandered. With the love they had for each other, their marriage could only last six months. No wonder Aisha and I couldn't even last a few months. Getting married is the root cause of misery for all men, I decided.

'We have company here,' he announced, breaking into my thoughts.

'I am sorry sir, what?'

'The second officer just called.' He nodded toward the phone. 'He's getting satellite warnings about pirate attacks in the vicinity.'

'Oh that,' I dismissed.

'I wouldn't worry too much,' he said airily. 'I've been here many times, never got caught.'

'Yeah, I'm sure we'll be okay,' I agreed.

'Okay,' he said, getting back on his seat and wiping his moist eyes. 'Let's just forget my past and move on. What about your story, what brings you guys on the brink of a divorce so early in your marriage?' A brief smile parted his lips.

It felt good to see him smiling after a long time. 'Aw sir,' I cried, 'let it be, you don't want to be hearing it.'

'No, I do,' he pressed. 'It sounds eerily similar to my story.'

I smiled. 'But before I do that you have to tell me something, sir.'

He nodded.

'Why do you still love her three decades after your divorce, and what had *happened* between you guys? You loved each other so much. And why do you feel so guilty about the whole thing? What did you do, sir?' I found the questions rushing out of my mouth.

'Oh dear, you'll know everything once I complete my story,' he replied leaning back in his chair. After a thoughtful glance at me, he added, 'you know when I look at you I think I see myself. I want to help you; I hope you are not making the same mistake as I did.'

What mistake?

I shook my head and forced a smile. 'So then sir, go on and complete your story. We'll know it then.'

'I'll do that,' he said, 'but first you must complete yours. My story might just end up inspiring you in the end, and well, who knows, you'll fall back in love with your wife...all over again.'

'Ha, ha, ha,' I laughed. 'You can be funny sir. That can never, ever happen.'

'Why not?' he asked. 'I could see you were madly in love with Aisha till then. I mean you yourself convinced everybody. Ha, ha, even your friend Joe for that matter. So what happened to all the love then?'

'I don't know sir about this love and all!' I shrugged. 'We were madly in love with each other for seven years before we got married and now...' I cleared my throat '...now there's everything, but love in our relationship. I think our marriage screwed it up. We shouldn't have married at all. Ours was a classic example of "From Yippee! We're getting married! to Why the hell did we get married? in seven flat days."'

'OK,' he said throwing out his arm, 'would you stop intriguing me and just tell me what happened? We don't have much time here, have to go on the bridge and take care of those Somalian bastards too.'

'Alright sir,' I slumped backward. 'This is a very tragic story, listen carefully.'

He threw a smile and waved at me to proceed.

19. YIPPEE! WE ARE MARRIED!
DAY – 1, February 2011, Delhi

I had never imagined life could be so wonderful. The warm sunshine percolating into our room, the trills of birdsongs, and a white smoke of mist outside made the morning ethereal. I had just woken up from one of my most satiating sleeps and rolled my eyes toward my wife. Aisha was still asleep beside me, her pretty face peeping out through the cosy blanket that wrapped her body.

We made love twice last night, then laughed and nattered through the entire night before falling asleep in each other's arms. Though I had barely slept a few hours, I felt fresh. We had a long last night and we reached our home way past midnight after our marriage. By the time we made our way to our room away from the prying eyes of a horde of my relatives in the living room, it was already three. And then we were on top of each other.

I moved closer to her and observed her closely. She appeared in complete harmony, still like a statue, save the occasional quiver of her eye lashes. A lock of hair sat on her cheeks, obscuring it, and I tucked it behind her ear. I resisted the urge of kissing her but found myself a minute later reaching for her, kissing her softly on her nose.

'Um…' she moaned. She parted her eyes with great difficulty surveying the surroundings and then shut them back again.

'Good morning, sweetie,' I said, stroking her hair gently. Even in the morning without washing her face she managed looking sensual.

'What time is it?' she croaked, scrunching up her nose.

'It's ten,' I replied. 'Mom has already called us twice, now get up, my relatives are waiting to bless the newlyweds.'

'Haven't they blessed us already in the night?' she asked peevishly. 'How much more do they want to bless?'

She covered her face with the blanket and turned over to the other side.

'Yeah, well, that's how they are, you know…' I craned my neck toward her to check if she was even listening, '…my relatives, they can never bless you enough.'

I waited for her to respond but could only hear her muffled snores from under the blanket a minute later.

'Oh, no, no…sweetie…you can't be sleeping now, they are waiting.' I shook her easily.

Silence.

'Hello…sweetie…get up baby…we have to get ready now.'

Silence.

'Aisha…baby…love you, please get up now.'

'*Alright!*' She threw the blanket in a fit of rage, rose, and steadied herself on the floor with her eyes shut. 'First you don't let me sleep in the night and then your damn relatives in the morning!' she said before marching toward the washroom.

God, she's so cute!

An hour later we made our way to the living room and all heads turned toward us.

I've always been very fond of my family and loved each one of them. My father has nine siblings – three brothers and six sisters – and together they share twenty three children amongst them. Over the years we have celebrated festivals, special occasions, and cricket matches together. We all have gone on quite a few family vacations during our summer holidays in school. With over forty people, our group had always been the largest and noisiest in trains, hotels or elsewhere. With close to two dozen cousins, I seldom felt the need of any friends, with the exception of Joe Singh, of course, who continues to be my best friend.

'Hey, there you are guys, the gorgeous couple,' shrieked Dimple aunty, my father's eldest sister. 'We have been waiting for ages for both of you.'

I reached out for her hands as we approached her. She hugged Aisha and whispered in my ear, 'had a great time last night?'

'Oh, come on, *bhua*,' I snorted. 'Don't embarrass me.'

'Ah,' she exclaimed, poking me in my chest, 'you little thug.'

'Aw, you got such a beautiful bride,' cried Sonam aunty from behind us, the youngest of all the siblings. She kissed Aisha on her cheeks. 'Great choice Ronit,' she said and thumped me lightly in my ribs.

'Thanks,' I said.

Over the next hour, my mother introduced her to everyone in the family. My sister Priya stood alongside her. She was seven years elder to me and had a six-year old son, Rohan, who had to be the most notorious kid alive. Unfortunately, my sister's marriage was in shambles as often she had fights with her in-laws. According to her, her husband wasn't supportive either. For this reason she didn't spend much of a time with them and was mostly at our place. Good for Aisha, I thought, she'll have good company.

As she met my relatives I could see that wide smile all over Aisha's face as she brought her hands together to greet them. For the older ones she'd bend down religiously touching their feet. My family would be so proud – a beautiful bride with all her traditional values intact. *Perfect!*

I could already see Aisha gelling along well with my family with long animated conversations interspersed with guffaws of laughter. Momentarily she'd glance over her shoulder toward me as if to thank me for the wonderful family I'd gifted her. I'd wink back at her, *you deserve the best baby!*

She loved each one of them, youngsters and the elders alike, I could sense by her demeanour. My family, after all, deserved to be loved. They were jovial, thoughtful, considerate, and more importantly loved having fun. Aisha would fit perfectly in this family, I could already see that.

When Aisha was done with my mother, I introduced her to my favourite cousins. She shook hands with them, tousled the hair of the kids, and shared jokes with them. Some of them asked about our love story, how we met and how it all began, and she rapturously narrated all of it. My cousins listened in rapt attention and I prided myself to be the hero of her story. Again I could see the love and adulation on her face for my cousins.

Apart from being a gorgeous looking woman, I decided, she had her heart in the right place. I mean not many women in this world would enjoy the company of her husband's family right from day one, but not Aisha. She was this gregarious woman, who despite negligible sleep, laughed and schmoozed with everyone and felt so confident and comfortable at the same time. I sat back in my chair and observed her revel in the long conversations.

Finally after what seemed like an eternity, she joined me on the adjacent chair. I wanted to hug her and thank her for being so warm and sociable with my family. I was sure she would want to do the same when she leaned toward me and whispered something in my ear. At first her words didn't register but when I rolled my eyes toward her, I was sure I heard them right. With a sudden livid look and bloodshot eyes, she asked:

'WHEN THE HELL ARE ALL THESE CLOWNS LEAVING?'

20. WOW, WE ARE MARRIED!
DAY – 2, Delhi

'Baby! Why have you been so angry with me all day?' I asked Aisha, latching the door of our room behind me, and slipping my feet out of the shoes. They had been aching badly as we had a long day.

We'd returned home from Suresh uncle's place – my father's eldest brother – in Malviya Nagar after dinner. The food menu was wide and delectable, the people were warm and courteous, and the drive back home was smooth and pleasant. If anything, she should have been delighted for a wonderful evening.

'You OK, baby?' I asked again, a little precarious this time. I could sense some cold vibes as she slipped out of her *sari* and then banged the door of the washroom behind her.

Okay. A lot of cold vibes.

I plopped over the bed and pondered over the day's events. *Was it something I had said? Or was it something I did?* I was sure I was the reason behind her sulky mood. Joe Singh had told me once: 'Whenever your woman is angry for no discernible reason, there could only be two things - either she was having her periods or her husband did or said something inappropriate.' I wondered how Joe Singh knew so much about women; the guy never even had a girlfriend. Mulling over his advice, I ruled out the first option. So then I began to ponder again, what had I done or said?

I fidgeted on the bed when she opened the door and made her way out with an exasperated sigh. She glowered at me from the corner of her eyes before leaning on her wardrobe. I sat tight-lipped and feigned calmness. A few minutes later when she was on the bed, I couldn't help and asked her again, 'Baby, is everything alright?'

'No!' she replied tartly and whisked through the magazine she picked from the side table beside her.

'At least tell me what happened?' I pleaded, squeezing her hands to draw her attention.

'Don't tell me you don't even *know*!' she said, shaking her head in agitation.

'No, I don't *know*,' I waved my arms out in defence. 'Would you mind telling me at least?'

She thumped the magazine back on the table and turned towards me. Her gaze bore through my eyes. 'Haven't you noticed we are not spending any time with each other? It's always your family first, isn't it? In the morning we were at Meenu auntie's place for lunch and then for dinner at Suresh uncle's and then tomorrow we would be going somewhere else. Why can't your relatives give us some space? I want to spend some "me time" with you. And then there are so many cousins and aunts and uncles and naked children in your house roaming around all over. I can't even move around freely here. Why can't they mind their own business and go back to their homes. Marriage is over, isn't it?'

'Oh baby, that's it,' I smiled, moving closer to her. 'I know, even I want to spend some alone time with you. Don't worry my relatives will leave in a few days anyway.'

'A few days?' she arched her brow.

'Aisha, don't get paranoid baby, I love you so much.' I held her arms and tugged her toward me.

'And what about your grandmother?' she asked, knocking my hands and pushing herself away from me. 'You know what she told me this morning?' Her face crumpled in a frown.

'What?' I asked, trying my best to hide the irritation in my voice.

'Get up in the morning before the sun rises, immediately take a shower, join me in the morning for the prayers, never call your husband by his name, start planning a baby-'

'OK, alright stop it,' I interjected. 'She's my grandmother, for heaven's sake. What do you expect from a woman her age?' I held her gaze expecting an answer. Instead she turned her face away.

'Alright Aisha, you don't have to follow everything what she says.'

'Not everything?' Her forehead furrowed as she faced me again. 'Really? So name a single thing she told me that I *can* follow? Getting up so early, not calling you by your name, what, tell me?' She placed her hand on her chin and glared back at me.

'Um…, I scratched my eyebrow. 'You could follow that… baby planning part, perhaps,' I replied with a coy smile.

Her shoulders fell and she didn't respond. She turned away and switched on the television. 'Yeah, well, come and hump me is all you can care.' She shook her head in disgust. 'I thought this guy was different,' she muttered under her breath.

'I *am* different,' I cried, feeling slightly insulted. 'And now I'll show you something you'll know I care.'

'Yeah, sure,' she said with an air of indifference gazing at the TV screen.

'Remember, how you used to tell me for the honeymoon you want to visit an exotic destination...' I trailed off, making it sink slowly, and waited for her reaction. She had told me a couple of times before our marriage that for the honeymoon she wanted to visit a place where she could see exotic mountains dotted with plantation and snow, pristine lakes adorning them offering a breathtaking view, indulging in activities like rock climbing and river rafting, away from the noisy and polluted cities that we have been brought up in.

A ghost of a smile played on her lips, but she tried hiding her curiosity. 'Yeah, what about that?' she asked casually, turning the volume of the TV down.

'Well,' I said, 'I've got something like that for us.' I slid open the drawer on my bed side and offered her two tickets. I had hidden them so it came as a surprise.

Her eyes widened in excitement and that sullen look vanished. 'Oh, are we going to *Switzerland*?' she asked with barely suppressed glee. 'I always wanted to visit that country,' she added leafing through the tickets.

No! Not Switzerland!

Her shoulders sagged in disappointment a moment later and her face became the colour of her red top that she was wearing. The anger returned. I wondered what was wrong when she caught me off guard with a scream. 'You are taking me to Nainital for the honeymoon?'

I couldn't amass the gall to look her in her eyes. Yes, I wanted to say, that's what matches the description with the place you have always described, but decided I was better off staying silent. I knew any words from me would fail me at this moment. When I looked at her again, a faint smile bordered her lips, and then later, it gave way to a hysterical laughter.

'Oh my God, I can't believe it!' she ran her hand through the few tendrils of her hairs that dangled over her face and pushed them back. 'Firstly you get me a honeymoon trip to Nainital and then you think I would be thrilled about it. And...' she waggled the tickets over my face, 'why are we taking a god damn bus for that godforsaken place, why can't we take a flight?'

'Because they don't have one um...an airport I mean,' I explained quickly. 'The nearest airport from Nainital is the Indira Gandhi International airport, and that's here, in Delhi.'

Thank God for that!

'Oh wow, great!' she said. 'Perfect.' She paused. '*By the way*, do you know I've been to that place at least ten times with my family and friends and now it'll be *so much fun* to go there again' - she gnashed her teeth and scowled - '*for my honeymoon!*'

I sealed my mouth shut.

She continued glaring at me. When she realized I had nothing else to offer she reached out to switch off the lights.

'GOODNIGHT!' she yelled before thrusting her back toward me.

'I love you, baby,' I said, snuggling up close to her.

She slammed her feet on my shin. 'DON'T TOUCH ME! GO AWAY!'

Oh boy, I so dreaded a platonic honeymoon.

21. THE PLATONIC HONEYMOON
DAY – 3, 4 & 5, Nainital

'You have ruined my honeymoon, I hope you know that,' she said as she gazed out of the window.

We were seated in a private bus on our way toward Nainital. The dark leather seats were high and comfortable, and the bus was almost full barring a few unoccupied seats. Outside, the weather was nice and balmy with the sun performing its morning ritual, ascending toward the stratus clouds, casting blazing streaks of sunshine across the window. Aisha had drawn the curtains slightly to prevent her skin from a tan.

We had crossed the Delhi border and the bus drove through the notorious streets of Uttar Pradesh in Bilaspur. The road was long and wide, flanked with dense forest on either side. Pine and oak trees lined the drive and the vegetation extended as far as the eyes could reach. Even from the distance I could see a dozen different shades of green and yellow.

'Did you not hear me?' she asked again, flipping her head toward me.

'I'm sorry, what?' I'd heard it.

She took a long breath and then exhaled sharply, almost making a snorting sound.

'You know a honeymoon is the most special vacation of any woman's life, something she would always cherish in the many years to come. I was so much looking forward to an exotic location and you know that…' She waggled her finger at me.

'Instead,' she continued sadly, 'you chose a place which I have already visited so many times with my parents. You have taken away "the special" part from my honeymoon. Any other time I would have loved coming here…' She paused, perhaps looking for the right words. 'So anyway, here's the deal' - she waved out her hand - 'now that you have ruined my honeymoon, I'll ruin yours.'

I stared at her blankly. 'What is that supposed to mean?'

'You men want only one thing…whether here in Nainital or elsewhere. It really doesn't matter to you, does it? So in this entire trip, no…' she curled her lips together to tease me '… yeah, you got it right, no love-making.'

'What?' I shuddered even at the thought. 'You're kidding, right?'

'Nope.' She raised her eyebrows with just a faint shake of her head. 'I'm not; tit for tat.'

'Tit for tat!' I almost screamed. 'You call it tit for tat?'

She didn't respond and appeared pleased at annoying me. She turned her gaze back outside the window.

'Hey.' I nudged her shoulder with my own. 'I thought you wanted to spend "me time" with me.' I took her hand in mine. 'Aren't we doing that?'

'Yeah,' she said, 'but I never said in *Nainital*. I had given you a hint so many times where I wanted to celebrate my honeymoon,' she replied freeing her hands from mine. 'And no touching as well.'

'Fine!' I said with a shade of asperity and looked away from her.

We didn't look at each other or spoke for the next few minutes until the bumpy ride began. The road was strewn with potholes and the damn driver refused to press the brakes. She turned her gaze back at me and as we held on to our seats steadying our self, she mouthed, 'PERFECT!' rolling her lips. I withdrew from her gaze and offered her a shrug.

The next hour went by quickly. I had closed my eyes and didn't realize I'd dozed off. When I woke up, I felt fresh and flexed my muscles. I squinted outside the window and a pleasant sight greeted my eyes. We had begun our ascent on the winding roads up on the hills. The roads were one-way and narrow, and until the bus rounded the corner, there wasn't any indication of the incoming traffic.

The sun had settled itself nice and high in the mountains, occasionally getting obscured and edging past the mountains offering oodles of sunshine. Below us a tiny river snaked past the foot of the mountains reflecting the indigo-blue of the cloudless sky above.

Aisha looked at me peering out and offered a faint smile. 'Woke up sleepy head?' she said tousling my hair.

I smiled back. It seemed to me her anger receded. 'Listen Aisha, I'm really sorry if this trip doesn't please you, I promise I'll take you to Switzerland next year.'

I took her hand in mine

'But why could you not now?'

She didn't let go off my hand this time.

'Because I didn't have enough money,' I said. 'Next time when I do I promise I'll take you there.' After a pause, I added, 'I love you baby and would never hurt you intentionally.'

She smiled under her breath. 'Okay, I believe you and...I love –'

The tension between us waned and I leaned forward to kiss her on her cheeks. She retracted suddenly and placed a finger on my lips.

'I love you too but as I said before no love making or even kissing in this trip,' she added cheekily.

I frowned and settled back in my seat.

We reached Nainital half past three. The driver had stopped once at a local restaurant for lunch. We ate scrambled eggs and bread as there was nothing much on the menu. From the bus stand we took a rickshaw for the hotel I had booked. My heart began pounding at the thought of her reaction hoping she would like it. Or rather love it.

She hated it.

'Here?' she screamed in horror as we stood on the road outside the "Hotel Grand". 'I thought you said we were staying in "The Grand".'

We were staring at an old, tawny coloured building which appeared to be built during the British era. Located on the mall road, it offered a panoramic view of the Naini Lake in front. And that's exactly what I thought while booking this place. You know, a nice romantic escapade, making love in the bed with a view of the lake and the hills in front.

Actually, there was another reason I booked it.

It was relatively cheap and I got a heavy discount through a reference.

'Oh gosh, it is only "Grand"!' I gasped and squinted my eyes through its board. 'Oh no, they cheated me, I was obviously booking "The Grand".' I turned my gaze toward her and she was still staring at the building in disgust. 'Shit, we don't even have a choice, I've already paid them. Now *we have* to stay here. Oh God no, why did this happen to us? Our honeymoon is screwed. I'll teach that travel agent a lesson once we are back home.'

Very slowly, she tilted her face toward me and gave me a cold stare. Her eyes were a fiery red, eyebrows raised, forehead creased, nose scrunched up, and for a moment I thought she had turned into a devil. After a full minute of that glare she replied, 'I'm sure it's not your fault, *you miserly old rat!*'

I cringed. I don't think she bought it.

And yeah, just so you know, there is no "The Grand" in Nainital.

An hour later we sat on wicker chairs in the balcony of the hotel overlooking the lake. We had ordered tea and snacks. Aisha was gazing toward the lake. Although the view was obscured by a few tall pine and oak trees sprawled along the road, the sight was still mesmerizing, especially when you have been living in a place like Delhi. The Mall road in front was thronged with tourists from all over the country. But still it was not as noisy as one would imagine.

Beyond the road, the Naini Lake - a slow moving mass of freshwater at the foot of the Kumaon hills - stretched either side till the eyes reached. It gleamed with shades of orange and yellow as it bathed in the generous sunshine. At night it would become a dark colour reflecting the charcoal sky above. In the distance I could see some boats paddling across it creating rippling waves behind them. Boating was one of the main leisure activities here and I had planned on one myself. Only if Aisha was interested, that is to say.

She finished her tea and without looking at me, headed for our room. Sensing the tension, I trailed behind her. I could almost hear her heels thudding past the floor as she headed to the washroom at the far end.

The room was large by any standards with neat marble flooring. The king size bed occupied one corner of the room, but sadly it wouldn't witness any love making in the night. A television screen nestled atop a beige wooden unit faced the bed in front. At its side was another wooden table offering a kettle, some tea bags, and sundry. So basically there was everything in the room which one would use and more. Why can women never be satisfied?

She came out with a bang on the door - her favourite gesture to portend anger - and then marched toward me. My throat tightened.

'First you get me to this dull place and then this hotel.' She threw up her hands and rolled her eyes. 'The least you could have done is booked a five star hotel so I could have enjoyed my stay and at least *something* would have felt special about this trip.' She let out a sigh of resentment and stared at me for an answer.

I buried my hands deep inside my pocket and shifted my weight nervously from one foot to the other. She continued glowering at me. I had to speak. Think...Something...The glare continued. OK, say anything...

'Sweetie, you know it was an honest mistake, I had booked The Gra–'

'Alright stop!' She thrust her hand almost in my face. The same, soft and beautiful hand I used to *once* hold lovingly. 'You think I'm a fool?'

I shook my head, and said, 'Sorry baby.'

She didn't react.

'Okay I'll tell you frankly.' I held her hand and ushered her toward the bed. We sat. 'Honestly, I hate spending money on hotels. And you know why?' I paused, hoping to get a... never mind. 'Because a five star hotel charges an exorbitant sum and more than half the time we are not even in the hotel, you know, doing shopping, sightseeing and all that. Besides I never think they are worth it. I would rather spend the money I save on shopping and...showering gifts on you, sweetheart.'

At that, I sensed her expression softened. Not much, though.

'Actually,' she said slowly, 'you know what? You're right. That somehow never occurred to me.'

'Thanks.' *Wow!*

'Give me your card then,' she held out her hand.

'What?'

'Give me your debit card then,' she said, flicking her fingers. 'Whatever money you have saved by making me stay here, I'll get something for myself in that much. Sounds like a fair deal to me.' Her expression was dead-pan. 'Good thinking, I must say,' she added slyly.

I stretched my arm slowly toward my back and pulled out the wallet from the back pocket of the jeans. She snatched it as soon as I got it forward.

'Thanks,' she uttered before waddling off to the balcony.

Can somebody please tell me what the hell just happened? The evening was beautiful. We were walking down the flea market on a road perpendicular to the Mall road. Darkness had set in early with a cloudless sky dotted with tiny white spots that twinkled at us. The temperature was mild and the air was filled with a thousand different and mellow sounds – a few children playing in the dusty playground, vendors selling eatables and artefacts, bells in the nearby temples, unwary customers bargaining while a few games like hoopla, shooting the balloons being played on the edge of the road. In the distance a gentle patter of the lake against its bank could be heard. A crisp breeze added to the serenity of the atmosphere.

We had returned from the boat ride and it was a pleasant experience, especially because Aisha appeared to be in an affable mood (perhaps due to my wallet in her hands). We had spent close to an hour on the boat and thankfully I felt the romance that had gone missing for the last few days, rekindle. Often in the boat we'd cup our hands, immersing them in the lukewarm water, and then splashed it over each other. She cowered down while giggling to avoid getting wet. Then she wrapped her legs close to her body and tucked her head inside while one arm fetched for the water which she stroked it in my direction constantly. But in the end I'd won comfortably.

Her smile hadn't faded ever since we left the boat and for a moment all seemed well with the world. With her wet hair and damp clothes she appeared more beautiful. I slipped an arm around her waist and she leaned into me, gracefully accepting my offer. I could smell the wonderful scent of her hair.

'I love you sweetheart,' I whispered the words in her ear, 'and I am the happiest person in the world for having you in my life.'

She looked up at me and a wide grin exposed her perfectly shaped teeth. 'Me too,' she blinked and then leaned further onto me.

I held her even more firmly. 'So what are you buying?' I dabbed at my wallet in her hands.

'Oh,' she thumped her forehead with her hand. 'I almost forgot about it.' She looked around her to decide what to buy.

Five minutes later she was still looking. Like my buddy Joe Singh tells me – 'Men go shopping to buy what they want; women go shopping to know what they want.' A classic example was right in front of my eyes. She had a hand around her chin and appeared lost in thoughts. I could almost imagine what she was thinking, *how do I blow up his damn money?*

'There!' She pointed toward a candle shop toward our right. 'We can start from there.'

'Sure.' I trailed behind her as she led me to the shop. *This is going to be so much fun!*

We came out after half an hour. She bought a dozen candles in the shapes of animals, birds, fruits and all sorts of weird shapes one would imagine. More importantly, I was poor by a close to five thousand rupees. I didn't utter a word.

Next, we stopped at an artefacts stall few hundred meters away from the first one. I asked her to carry on and waited outside. She returned after another thirty minutes. My face fell at the sight of her full hands. I took the packets from her and from the corner of my eyes flicked through the bill in her hands. It said 6530 rupees *only*. I didn't utter a word.

As we walked down the Mall road, there was a wide variety of garment shops sprawled along the road. She stopped at one of them. But I didn't flinch, I was sure she wouldn't pick anything as she was very choosy about her clothes.

She did pick; some seven, eight of them and then thrust the packets on me. She appeared thrilled with herself and almost patted herself for a job well done. I badly wanted to but didn't utter a word.

As we walked down the road toward our hotel I couldn't help but wonder about a niggling thought in my mind.

Did I really tell her that I am the happiest man in the world for having her?

We reached our room twenty minutes later. Something had been bothering me and I gushed out the moment I opened the door. I did realize my folly few minutes later though.

'You spent over fifteen thousand rupees in an hour?' I shook my head in amusement. 'And just like that,' I added clicking in the air twice.

'Yeah.'

'Yeah…yeah,' I imitated her with an air of disgust. 'That's all you have to say.'

She threw the packets on the bed and swirled around to face me. 'So what did you tell me this afternoon, huh?' I didn't look at her as she recounted my words. 'Save money… shopping…showering gifts on me. So like any good wife that's exactly I was doing, following the orders of my dear husband.'

'Yeah, alright,' I said, 'but not one…two…three…*fifteen thousand rupees!* Are you completely insane? I mean no one blows money like that. It takes a lot of hard work to earn it, but how would you know, huh? You have never earned a single penny all your life and would never do so. *I'm here for that, isn't it?'*

She drew a long breath and then shook her head. 'I don't believe this...you are actually shouting at me for...money. All you guys are the same.' She poked a finger in my chest. 'Priyank was right.'

'What?' I asked curiously. Suddenly something felt funny and I chuckled. '*Priyank* was right...that all *you guys* are the same...isn't he one himself?' I *had* to tell this one to Joe Singh.

'Okay, stop grinning,' she ordered. 'Don't you dare make fun of my brother.'

I smiled. 'I didn't even say a word about him.'

She turned her gaze away from me. When she held my gaze again, her face was puckered in a frown. 'I still can't believe you guys put toothpaste in his ass. What kind of a psycho does that?'

At that I laughed out loud. 'Now what has that got to do with this conversation? Do you girls ever forget anything or what?' I dismissed with a shake of my head. 'And by the way he reciprocated that gesture...thrice,' I added quickly.

'Well, ha, ha...my brother always wins,' she replied before trudging down the hallway toward the washroom.

And there it was again...that bang!

Next morning was a haze of memories. Sunlight poured into our room when I rose up on my feet from the couch adjacent to the bed. Yes, the couch. She kicked me out of the bed last night and said I didn't even deserve to sleep with her.

While she was asleep, I had decided our schedule for the day and the list of places we would see. We'd start our day with the

Naina Devi Temple located on the northern shore of the Naini Lake and offer our prayers, perhaps to steady our relationship. Since Aisha loved animals, a visit to the Govind Ballabh Pant zoo was a must. That might just make her less angry. I also wanted to the visit the Governor's house or the Raj Bhawan. I'd heard it consisted of some 113 rooms and even a golf course. A visit to the snow view point offering a panoramic view of the Himalayan range like Nanda Devi, Trishul and Nanda Kot via a cable car was next on the list. We'd have lunch over there at one of the restaurants overlooking the hills, engage in a little mischief, romance a bit and, get our photographs clicked. And if time permitted, we'd also visit the Eco Cave Garden, Tiffin's top and the Land's end which I heard offer a splendid view of the neighbouring country side and the hills.

By late evening, while returning to the hotel, she'd fall in my arms, and then well, who knows, she might just change her decision of no lovemaking in the honeymoon.

I wish I could say that everything went the way I'd planned, except that it didn't. You see there was just a little problem. Aisha disagreed to budge from the hotel. She said something like she didn't want to go anywhere with a moron who shouted at his wife for no reason. So I spent my entire day watching television and Aisha…actually where *was* Aisha?

The next morning we boarded the bus to Delhi from the designated location after she finished packing in a huff. By late evening we were looking for an auto rickshaw in Delhi, back to our place.

And with that, came an end to the most 'uneventful' honeymoon in the history of honeymoons.

22. OKAY, WE ARE MARRIED NOW!
DAY – 6, Delhi

I spent the entire day out with my cousins, as honestly, I wanted a break from my nagging wife. When they asked about her, I simply replied she wasn't well. We watched a 'Priyanka Chopra' movie in PVR Select-City walk in Saket and had lunch at Pizza Hut. As they enquired about our honeymoon and I slowly recounted the relevant parts, a thought struck me that I wasn't even missing her.

When I reached home in the evening, a few of my relatives from my mother's side were there. Aisha was cooking dinner in the kitchen with our maid. I don't know why she was even trying? She had to be the most awful cook I had ever known. I mean how could someone manage to ruin the taste of even our ageless 'Maggi noodles'?

I extended my greetings to my relatives and tottered toward the kitchen. I was damn hungry. My sister and Aisha apparently were helping our maid. My mother was in the living room entertaining her guests. As I whisked my eyes through the dishes, wondering what to eat, I couldn't help but notice Aisha didn't even look my way, as though I was a stranger. Priya observed the cold vibes between us and glanced at me and her back and forth a couple of times.

'Aisha what's wrong with you?' she asked. 'Your husband is here and you don't even look at him.'

With a faint shake of her head she glanced at me. 'You can take something if you like,' she offered.

Priya was taken aback. 'That's it?' She forced a smile. 'That's all you are going to say. You know, Aisha, if I behave like this in my husband's home, they'll throw me out of there.'

'Okay, let it be, Priya,' I interjected. 'Don't bother; I'm not that hungry anyway. I'll have dinner later.' I walked out the kitchen and let the two women at it.

'Never interfere in women's affairs, especially if they were related to you,' Joe Singh once told me. 'You'll end up antagonizing both of them'. Behind me I heard their petty argument with Priya dominating all the way.

We had dinner an hour later. My relatives had left in spite of my mother badgering them to have dinner with us. They had other plans. Good for us.

On the dining table I could sense those cold vibes between Aisha and Priya now. My stomach churned. Oh, it wasn't a good feeling; it wasn't a good feeling at all! I could sense from Aisha's sulky expression, a long lecture awaited me in my room later. Again!

'Oh!' My grandmother threw up on her plate. 'This maid has ruined the taste of *bhindi*.'

The mush sat on her plate much to our disgust.

'Ha, ha, ha, oh gosh,' Priya laughed.

'What's funny?' I asked.

'*Dadi,*' she replied, ignoring me, 'the maid has not made that. That masterpiece is the work of' - she threw a nasty look at Aisha - 'your sweet grand-daughter-in-law, ha, ha.'

'Ew!' Mom made a face through a mouthful. 'It's horrible.'

'Ha, ha, ha,' Priya laughed again.

Aisha glared at her. 'Thanks for the encouragement,' she whispered under her breath before glancing at me.

'What?' Priya said. 'What did you just say?'

Aisha shook her head slowly. 'Nothing.'

'You know Aisha,' she continued, 'if I behave like that in front of my in-laws and husband, he would have divorced me long time back. You should be taught some manners.'

Aisha said nothing. She just threw me a look. *Oh boy!*

Right then a thought crossed my mind that in the last five days not even a single day passed when my wife wasn't angry with me, or wasn't in a cranky mood, or didn't complain about something I did or said. In short, we didn't spend a span of twenty four hours cordially with each other as we did before marriage. I was sure after dinner this would be the sixth straight day.

My thoughts were interrupted by my grandmother's statement. 'Aisha, you must accompany me in the morning *aarti* from tomorrow onwards. These two ladies' - she motioned toward my mother and Priya - 'are too lazy for it. But no excuse from you, huh,' she declared without expecting an answer.

Aisha nodded submissively. Priya laughed as my mother looked on.

The door to our room creaked open an hour later and an uneasy feeling gripped me. She entered our room and headed straight toward the washroom. No bang...thankfully.

I leafed through a magazine on the couch and shifted the remote of the television to her side of the bed so she had something to do other than yell at me. When she came out of the washroom, without a bang again, she carried on with her chores slowly – from the ironed clothes separated hers from mine, neatly stacked them in our respective wardrobe, changed the bed sheet and set the pillows, arranged the room in general. I took that as a good sign. However, from the corner of her eyes, I could sense she was expecting something from me - an explanation about…something, perhaps an apology or some discussion or attention.

Ten minutes later after her poker-face expression had nothing to offer, I thought of indulging in some conversation. That was important, you see, otherwise next time she'd lecture me – 'you are so insensitive and don't even care why I'm in a bad mood.'

You are a woman, what else? I should probably tell her.

'It's a bit cold today,' I said, making my way toward our bed.

'Em…' she said, switching the television on. She lied down next to me and pulled the blanket over.

I waited for her to continue. She didn't.

'*7 Khoon Maaf* is a good movie.'

She tilted her head toward me, and said, 'You didn't even ask me if wanted to come along.' From her tone, it didn't come as a complaint, just a general statement. Was it the lull before the storm?

I took a moment to answer. 'Aisha, you have been mad at me for the last two days,' I said as politely as I could. 'You would have never accompanied me anyway.'

'So that means you'll give up on me, huh?' she said quickly. I sensed a tinge of sadness in her voice. 'Would you not console me or persuade me like you used to do before marriage?'

I kept the magazine aside and took a deep breath. 'I don't know Aisha, but things are not working smoothly between us for the last few days. I mean, you get upset with almost anything I do, anything I say.'

'Ronit!' she said. 'Please try and understand. I have left my city where I've been born and brought up for you; my home and my entire family for you. Don't you think I'll have some expectations?' She propped herself on her elbows and faced me directly. 'I wanted a special honeymoon, agreed you said you didn't have money, then you booked us in an ordinary hotel and on top of that you yelled at me for shopping. I mean, now I don't even have any right to spend your money, is it?' She paused for an answer.

I didn't reply. How deftly she has manoeuvred back in lecture mode?

'Your sister,' she continued, 'gives me such crap about marriage. I should be telling her look at you first. Hasn't she ruined her own? And you were there on the dining table but didn't say a word in my defense. And you know today, like you, your sister and mother had left me alone in the house with her notorious kid Rohan and your grandmother. Why can't she take Rohan along to her kitty parties? Why not, huh? Tell me?'

Now this time I had to answer as she refused to withdraw her gaze from mine. I slowly ran my hand through my hair.

'Sweetheart...,' I said, '...please understand! He's a very naughty kid. Priya and mom have a tough time handling him.'

'So they'll thrust him on me, is it?' she howled. 'You know how that six year old harassed me today?'

I slowly shook my head. 'Please enlighten me.'

'Of course,' she said, 'I'll *enlighten* you. That kid broke some of my cosmetics including perfumes, lipsticks and moisturizers. He drew patterns across our dressing mirror with my' - she gritted her teeth - '*lipstick* which took me over an hour to clean. And then when I scolded him, he screamed his lungs out. He's got such a high-pitched scream; you have to hear it to believe it. Then when he realized I was getting irritated by it, purposely huh, purposely, he leaped toward me and screamed in my ear. You know my ears are still ringing by that pesky noise of his. Then when I again scolded him he held my hair and yanked at it. He's got such strong hands he managed to uproot few of my strands. Can you believe it? Oh God! I hate that kid '

'And your grandmother!' she continued after a grunt. 'She's no less by the way, huh. She's hell-bent on having a grandchild right away. You know she said start trying immediately when Ronit returns home today. I mean, who does she think I am?' She paused to draw a breath of contempt. 'But still, you know, I'm ready to face all this because...I love you. The least I can expect is some love and support from you as well. Instead what do you do - you leave me all alone in the house and go for a movie with your cousins. Now tell me is that right on your part? And now from tomorrow I have to be up early so I can join your grandma for prayers. I hate getting up early, you know it. Can't you do something about it, please?'

'Oh baby,' I said, 'come on, that won't be much of a problem, you see, after the first few days...you'll get used to getting up early anyway.'

'Oh God!' Her shoulders fell and she thumped her forehead with the heel of her palms. 'Really, *that's* the solution I can expect from you! You'll get *used* to it!' Her thunderous voice was back and her face slowly curled into a grimace.

'See I know you are right,' I quickly added to appease her, 'but I don't want to be sandwiched between you women. Please handle my sister or my mother or for that matter even my grandmother on your own. I don't want to be fighting with them over you, it's gonna get really ugly. If you have a problem with *me;* tell me, I'll do whatever I can to work on it, but not them, please try and understand.'

'*Okay, fine!*' she said. 'But what about you? Why do *you* have to be so inconsiderate all the time? Why can't you do something…anything that makes me feel good, so that I feel… that you still love me?'

I smiled. 'Sure baby, anything for you, but…what do you want me to do?'

She rolled her eyes. 'Flatter me! Praise me! Throw up a few surprises for me! Get presents for me, you know like gold, clothes, perfumes, anything. Be more supportive and caring! Take me dining to good restaurants! There is so much you can do to make me feel good; I can't believe you're actually asking me that.'

I replied after a thought. 'Okay then, I'll get a fixed deposit done in your name; sounds good to you?'

'*What!* You'll get me a goddamn FD? What do you want me to do with that, huh, hang it from my bloody ears like an earring or what? Get me something in gold if you can't even decide.'

Another thought crossed my mind. 'Okay, will do baby,' I said, 'but not before you give me a tight hug.'

She smiled and leaped in my arms, 'Wow, so you'll really get me some gold.'

I nodded and reached for her lips. We kissed slowly.

Well, it's not *that* difficult to keep a woman happy, is it?

23. WHY THE HELL DID WE GET MARRIED?
DAY – 7, Delhi

Last night was amazing - we finally made love.
Hopefully those times we shared before our marriage would return. To ensure that they did, indeed, first thing in the morning I found myself at our family jeweller. I wanted to show Aisha I truly cared for her and hence wanted to fulfil her wish right away. She wanted something in gold, so here I was, buying *something in gold* for her.

On my way back home I was glad and content. This would be the perfect gift for her. I'd got it packed neatly so while she opened it I could watch the nuances in her expression. Hopefully she'd squeal with happiness and hug me…we would make love…again…and then again.

No, it isn't difficult to keep a woman happy; I finally decided the answer to the question that popped up in my head last night.

'What the hell is wrong with you?' she screamed while staring at my gift in bewilderment. 'You got me this?' She threw the two gold biscuits at me. 'Where do you want me to hang this damn thing, around my neck or my bloody ears?'

What is wrong with her? Buying gold biscuits is the best

form of investment, besides there is no expenditure on its fabrication. Women, I tell you.

'Don't you...like it?' I asked slowly as I cradled the biscuits in my hands. They sparkled and were pretty, and I loved the feeling of their touch in my hands. 'You said you wanted... something in gold,' I added.

'*You insensitive pig!*' she yelled with gritted teeth. With a violent shake of her head, she stormed out the room with big, thudding steps, and a deafening bang of the door behind her.

Why pig?

Later that evening, I got another heavy dose of reprimand. You see, a few days before marriage my sister had borrowed some money from me which she said she'd return in a few months time. Like any doting brother, I was happy to assist her and never asked the reason for the same.

Then today I found out the reason in the most disconcerting way I had ever imagined when I heard another bang of the door. Honestly, I was fed up now.

'You gave your sister one lakh rupees so she could have a vacation in Dubai?' I heard the sharp squeal from a familiar voice.

I wasn't even looking in that direction.

'And when I asked you for it, you said you have no money to go for *our* honeymoon. You blabber about getting me a damn fixed deposit, get me gold biscuits which I should rightfully shove up your ass - your favourite sport - as I specifically said I wanted earrings...'

Okay, firstly how many times will she torment me for that 'ass thing', and secondly, she was NOT specific about the earrings.

'…but you don't have money for *our* honeymoon?'

She scowled at me through those blazing red eyes which made me fall in love with her few years back. How times change?

After a few unsettling minutes I decided to answer. I'll never forget this moment for the rest of my life, for what happened then, and the realization that followed in the next few days, shook my entire world. I said something like this, I think: 'You are always yelling at me Aisha. What do you even want?'

'What do I even want?' she repeated, crossing her arms against her chest, and thrusting one leg out. 'Well I'll tell you what I want. What I want is a caring, supportive and loving husband who doesn't buy me gold biscuits so it can be a *fair investment* for him. Instead he showers gifts on me and flatters me with a lot of surprises. He should be courteous and polite, love me and be kind like *you* were before marriage. I want him to be sensitive and listen to my problems attentively and then solve it and not give me some crap that I won't interfere in *you* women. I want him to spend maximum time with me and next time his sister is rude to me, he stands by me…'

The tune of the famous song, 'stand by me' played in my head. What a song it was by John Lennon. I just love that song. They didn't do justice to its Hindi adaptation, however, in the movie *Ra One*. Somehow I didn't like that movie too much. Shahrukh wasn't at his best but Kareena looked ravishing. Saif is a lucky guy.

'...I want him to respect me, my feelings, and my desires, and then fulfill each one of them. I want him to understand the sacrifices I have made for him by leaving my family. I want him to be a good friend, a good companion, and most importantly a man. I want him to be a good listener, be warm, sympathetic, funny, tender, tolerant, understanding, courageous, dependable...'

I love 'Mr. Dependable' or 'The Wall' of our cricket – the great batting legend Rahul Dravid. He is one of the finest batsmen India has ever seen. I simply adore his technique and perseverance when he is all padded up. Speaking of cricket, World Cup 2011 has just begun few days back. Wonder whose match it is today. I have a gut feeling India will win the cup this time. After twenty eight long years! Wow! I'm not even that old, huh! I should be a ship captain by that age, hopefully. We'll see.

'...passionate, compassionate and honest. I want him to sometimes help me in the kitchen and not merely order what he wants to eat. And after his meals, he should pick up his own damn dishes and place them in the sink not before spraying some water over them...'

Where is the remote, I can't find it...oh there. What is it doing on the bed? After she's done with her blah...blah...blah I must switch the TV on. Don't want to miss if it's India's match...OK, let me listen to at least some of what she's saying. She might ask me later and if I can't answer...well, well, well, another damn lecture. She said be a good listener or something like that...Hang on! Why are there horns over her head? God, when did she have long, piercing teeth protruding out from her mouth, and why are her eyes so red? Let me rub my eyes... oh, no, just something in my head.

'…I don't want him to put his wet towel on the bed and certainly not on the floor. His shoes should lie neatly in the shoe rack so I don't stub my feet over them and slip every day and the socks should go in the laundry bag and *never* on the floor, definitely not on the bed and *not* over the TV. He *should not* throw his clothes on the bed and expect his mother to put it in the wardrobe for him and certainly not me. I am a wife, for god's sake, not someone's servant or mother. I don't care how yucky my food is; he must eat it, enjoy it, and then compliment me for it, as at least I'm trying. He should not behave like a mamma's boy who can only enjoy food cooked by his mother.'

Oh, why are those horns, protruding teeth, and red eyes back? Am I imagining something…or is it really there?

'…I can wake up any time in the morning, take a shower when I want, wear any god damn clothes in the house and no one should tell me anything. Other than that I want him to compliment me frequently and not give me any stress.' For a very brief moment, she paused. 'That's all. Now, is that too hard?'

I stared at her. My God, is she done? My stomach gurgled. I wanted to laugh and laugh and laugh, and then some more. But more importantly, I wanted the answer to the question that had been ringing in my head all this while.

Was my wife turning into a devil?

24. YES, MY WIFE IS A DEVIL
March 2011, Delhi

It was sometime in March, just a few weeks after my marriage, when I was fully convinced that my wife had transformed into a devil. Nothing profound happened though; it was the chain of events that transpired which affirmed my belief.

Not even a single day passed after that day of 'I'll tell you what I want' lecture when my wife didn't have something to nag about. She had over a gazillion topics to pester me spanning my mother, sister, grandmother, Rohan's misbehaviour or my own, for that matter. It could be my getting up late in the mornings or coming back late at night; it could be my untidy wardrobe, untidy shoe rack or wet bathroom floor; it could be my appearance, my 'unhealthy' eating habits, my snoring or my negligence. It could be any and so many things, but I never bothered now. I thanked God every day for he gave us two ears.

But there was one thing common in all those rebukes. Whenever I looked at her, those familiar set of horns, piercing teeth jutting out of her mouth, blazing red eyes framed her appearance. It was always a vivid and constant image and never wavered like it did the first time last month. Her rough, dishevelled hair scrambled all over her face and those fingers wagged at me always had long, crooked nails. Her hoarse voice trembled its way out in a rage and sometimes the eye sockets went missing exposing a deep red colour behind. Then later her sallow skin always morphed to a bright red after the argument; the devil was done sucking my blood.

Thankfully, World Cup 2011 was in progress and I had the perfect excuse to slip out of the house. Like all women, she hated cricket. I didn't watch it in my room on the pretext that, 'Oh baby you'll be disturbed.' Initially she was very pleased with my concern for her but later when she realized it was my modus operandi to be away from her...you know what!

So every afternoon I found myself at some of my cousins' or friends' place. We had a great time – enough beers to last the match and our favourite chicken snacks to go along with them. Then late in the night I'd be home and would tiptoe my way towards the bed making minimal noise so as not to wake my devil, my wife I mean. But at times when I was a tad too loud and she did wake up...you know what!

But life wasn't too bad; half the day went outside the house and the other half almost on bed. Only the few hours in between were bad. Sometimes on my good days I scraped through the entire day unscathed - no nagging, no criticism and no arguments!

A few days after the realization (that my wife is a devil) as I approached my house one Sunday, I heard two women bickering inside. I instantly recognized the two voices and tottered inside to sort out the mess.

'Aisha!' Priya bellowed. 'If I behave like you behave in my house, my in-laws would have thrown me out!'

'Oh, would you stop giving me that crap every time!' Aisha said. 'Look at yourself, living with us. Don't you see it; they have anyway thrown you out!'

'How dare you talk to me like that? This attitude of yours will not be tolerated in this house, you get it?' Priya yelled at a furious looking Aisha.

As I made my way toward them to resolve the issue, Joe Singh's words dawned on me – 'Never interfere in women's affairs'. As good sense prevailed, I hid behind the door and peeped occasionally.

'Oh really,' Aisha said, 'and who exactly are you to tell me this, you don't even belong to this house anymore.'

'I'm the daughter of this house, you *bimbo*!' Priya replied, gnashing her teeth. 'You'll do exactly what we tell you to do, this is *our* house.'

'Oh, how dare you call me a bimbo?' Aisha said, looking at mom for intervention. 'Let Ronit come and I'll tell him what's going on here, how you ill-treat me. He'll make sure your entry is banned in this house.'

I rolled my eyes and looked upward. *Why God?*

Priya laughed. 'He'll ban *me* from entering this house, his own sister,' she said thumping her hand over her chest. 'Oh dear, *now* let him come, I'll tell him to throw *you* out, the root of all the problems.'

'Yeah, sure, we'll see,' Aisha howled. She turned toward mom. 'Why don't you say anything to her, just because she is your own daughter?'

Mom took a moment to answer. 'Look Aisha,' she said calmly, 'you have left your own house to live with your husband and us. There are certain norms of this house; you have to follow them so everyone lives peacefully.'

'But mom,' Aisha said, throwing out her arms, 'why do I have to baby sit Rohan all the time?' She gnashed her teeth and faced Priya, 'This is the fourth time she's asking me for this favour in the last one month. I can't tolerate that kid. Why can't she take him along with her? Is she *ashamed* of her own child or what?'

'Hey!' Priya groaned, thrusting a hand in Aisha's chest. 'Watch your words, you bitch!'

Aisha staggered backward and struggled to avert a slip.

I watched the drama in complete dismay from a distance, clear in my head, any action by me would cause an equal and opposite reaction. Needless to say, I stood my ground.

'Oh! How dare you!' Aisha took a step forward and thrust both her arms violently over Priya watching her stumble over the floor. '*You!*' she said, wagging a baleful finger at Priya, 'watch your words.'

In an instant, Priya rose to her feet and pushed Aisha who reciprocated the gesture. Seconds later the scene became uglier with both of them slapping and kicking each other. My grandmother came rushing out of her room with the commotion and her eyes were met by a wall-eyed mom. I stood hiding behind the wall with a mouth that refused to shut.

Both of them kept screaming, 'You bitch!' and pushed each other, and it was then when it became the ugliest. They began yanking each other's hair and whined in pain. And just then, it happened.

Aisha stared at the object in her hands with a gaping mouth and then glanced at Priya. Confusion swept past her face which later broke into a smile. Seconds later she was laughing uncontrollably. 'Oh my God!' said Aisha. 'You're…bald, ha, ha, ha, and, you…you wear a wig. Oh God, I have to take your picture and upload it on facebook, ha, ha, ha.'

Priya rooted her eyes to the ground and couldn't hide her embarrassment. Her glum expression didn't stop Aisha from giggling.

A minute later when Aisha refused to calm down, mom took a step forward, and hurled her arm across her face. 'Don't you dare make fun of my daughter, do you get it?'

'But mom,' Aisha said, wiping the tears from the back of her hands, 'she is the one who starte-'

'Just shut up!' mom hissed. 'And get out of here!' She threw out her arm to our room's direction.

Slowly, Aisha turned around making her way out.

'And one more thing,' mom called out. 'Next time *never* tell Priya this is not her house. Of course this is her house!'

Aisha trudged toward our room dejectedly.

I turned around and walked the other way, down the street. I shouldn't be going in there for some time, a few days perhaps.

'Oh, thank God you have come,' Aisha said, lifting her head from her knees. Her legs were tugged close to her body and arms wrapped around them. Her eyes were wet and pudgy, perhaps from all the crying since the last two hours. Her voice was hollow and there was a careworn edge to it. 'Where have you been all this while?'

'Have you been crying?' I asked, ignoring her question, closing the door behind me. 'What happened?'

'Your bloody sister, what else?' she replied, wiping her tears. 'You know how much she abuses and ill-treats me? Why can't she stay in her own house? And your mother also doesn't support me; you know she *slapped* me today. What is this Ronit?'

I rested my forehead in my arms. 'Why can't you just ignore her,' I said. 'I mean just take it from one ear and out from the other.' *Like I do*, I wanted to add.

'And *that's* the solution I expect from my supporting husband?' She raised her eyebrows. 'Oh God, why did I ever get married?'

I tutted and withdrew from her gaze.

'Why can't you ever be supportive Ronit?'

I turned my gaze back at her. And there, it was back – the horns, crooked nails, blazing red eyes, and piercing teeth.

'Why don't you care about me anymore?' she said, running her hand over her eyes. 'Your sister orders me to babysit her stupid son so she can have a good time outside. You also leave me alone in the house every day, where you go, what you do, I have no clue. Your mother slaps me in front of everyone; if I don't listen to them I'm warned I'll be thrown out of the house, and you' - she made a face, gritting her teeth - 'Don't even bother about anything! You only care about your food and your damn World Cup!'

I bit on the last bit of chicken *seekh* that clung between my teeth. Hmm…nothing beats a cold beer and hot chicken kebabs. 'Khan Chacha's' food is delightful and I always find it much better than its counterpart 'Bade Miya' of Mumbai. Tomorrow I'll try *tangri* kebab, another of his specialties. Or probably a chicken roll, but I'll tell him to put some more green chutney and onions in it; he had put it sparingly last time.

'…but you were not like this before marriage. You have changed completely now. All you care about is your family; I'm the least of your priorities. Do you even love me now? I doubt it. You don't even take me out for dinner or a movie. I'm always stuck in this house with your stupid family. And I know what you'll be thinking now: another day, another lecture. Why can't she ever be quiet, what is wrong with her? Maybe…'

No, I wasn't thinking about that now. In fact, I wasn't thinking anything. I was just noticing the straw that pierced my arm and lead straight to her mouth. In between her hoarse tone she'd suck on it and gulped down my blood. No wonder, I was getting leaner day by day while her skin a tomatoey colour. With a hesitation I glanced at her. She went on haranguing me and I was struck by that frightening look. Those red eyes were damn scary, the horns over head quivered back and forth with the movement of her body, and a messy lock of bedraggled hair flew down her face failing to hide those long and jagged teeth jutting out of her mouth.

'WHAT?' the devil grunted. 'Where are you lost? Are you even listening to me?'

'Y..y..e…s..s..s, I….a..m…' I floundered.

Later that night, during my fitful sleep, a thought occurred to me. Did I make a mistake getting married?

Of course! came the abrupt answer.

25. WHO CAN YELL LOUDER?
April 2011, Delhi

In the coming days, our marriage went from bad to worse. I could sense things changing in front of my eyes but couldn't do anything about it. We slept miles apart on the bed, seldom talked, our eyes hardly met - when they did it was more for obligatory reasons than for affection, like how many *chapattis* will you have, when would you be back home, et cetera – and sex was definitely out of question.

One Sunday morning in the month of April, I slowly sipped coffee in my room and wondered where our marriage was headed. Aisha quietly arranged the wardrobe toward my right. I could tell from her demeanour, her mind was elsewhere.

'Ronit, um…,' she began. My throat tightened. 'I was just wondering if we could shift to a new home, you know where no one else is around.'

'Why would you say that?' I asked, looking up and meeting her eyes. 'What is the problem here?' I didn't even remember when was the last time I looked at them, probably last Saturday when I yelled at her and gave her a piece of my mind.

'You don't see any problem here?' she said, raising her voice by an octave.

She always began softly but the conversation would always culminate with her yelling. I wasn't too far behind in that now. I had some male ego after all. Every morning, every afternoon, every evening, the devil had something to bicker about. Then last Saturday I completely lost it and yelled back at her causing thick tears to emerge from her eyes. That didn't deter me and I continued my rant. All I told her was to maintain cordial relations with my sister for a few more weeks. Things were finally settling in at her place and she would move out of our house. She was anyway depressed with her own marriage falling apart and a kid, the least you can do is give her that consideration, I told her. To this she said why does mom not take her side at least? My mother was obviously worried about Priya and so naturally she always took her side. But Aisha had a problem with that as well.

I asked her to keep her anger to herself and just be polite with both of them. To this she yelled back asking why she should be taking Priya's nonsense.

There we go again. So I yelled back louder, 'Did I not tell you the reason just now? Because she's having problems in her own house, you bimbo, do you never understand?'

And then she sobbed louder.

Why do women never understand? I have lived with them for twenty-five years, how can I not support them for a woman I have known just seven years? And isn't marriage all about compromises. She keeps flagellating me with her bullshit of what she expects from me, what a woman wants, how a good husband should behave and related crap, then why doesn't she get this little thing. That's the *only* thing I want from her. Only thing *any* married man wants as opposed to the long list of women.

So what does she do the next day - she tells my grandmother if Priya can't get up in the morning for the prayers, even she can't. And there was a tinge of rudeness in her voice as per my mother who narrated the incident to me that evening. So again, we had another fight, and I yelled at her. That yelling did another thing. It made the devil disappear, only temporarily though, as she was not the one who would stay quiet. With her yelling, the devil always returned but with my counter yelling, it disappeared. So lately we had started playing this little game I liked to call, 'Who can yell louder?'

'HEY! You don't see *any* problem here?' she repeated when she observed I wasn't listening.

Of course, the devil was back and so was the squelching sound of the straw.

I tried suppressing my fury. I didn't want to be increasing my blood pressure every now and then and get a damn heart attack. I understood then, the primary reason for heart attacks amongst men. Women!

'Alright Aisha, look,' I said. 'Firstly, I don't have money to get a house for myself, and secondly, even if I had, *we are not moving out from here!*'

Damn, the devil was out.

She fell silent and looked around glumly. 'So now, you'll be deciding everything, right? I don't even have *any* say in our matters now?' She pouted her lips and glared at me.

Damn! It was back. I could hear the squelching sound of her gnarled lips against the straw that penetrated my arm from the other end. The horns and her jagged teeth stared at me, threatening…warning to pierce my flesh.

'Aisha!' I said. 'Why the hell are we even discussing this? You know that's not possible. Why don't you get it, moving out of the house is not the solution. *You* have to change your attitude. Marriage is not just about two people; it's also about *accepting one's family!* I loved as she recoiled at my last three words.

'Oh really!' she said, nodding her head indignantly. 'Talking about accepting one's *family? When was the last time you met my parents or even gave them a call, tell me?*'

The squelching sound grew louder.

'Oh God!' I dragged myself out of bed in a huff. 'How do your parents *even come to the picture here?* That's entirely different.' I cleared my throat and rooted through the drawer for cigarettes. Yes, I started smoking after my marriage. Perhaps she would gift me a heart attack for our first anniversary. *'We are not even staying with them!'*

'Oh, so that is different, how so?'

I stared at her...just stared at her. How the hell did the argument even reach her parents? That was the thing with Aisha. She'd always start an argument and then drift to an irrelevant topic losing track of what the issue really was.

I shook my head violently and reached for the door. After walking out of the room, I banged it loudly against the wall. I opened it again and then banged it one more time, then one more time, and then one last time.

Damn, the devil disappeared.

A beautiful lady appeared at our door the next week. I was surprised by the unexpected visitor. She greeted me with a flushed expression. Her hair was short and neatly combed. The lady wore light blue denims that fell on blue canvas shoes. Her top was – Damn! - a baby pink colour.

'Oh brother!' Aisha leaped toward the door to hug her, I mean him. 'So glad you came.'

'Of course, sister,' Priyank said, embracing her and gnashing his teeth at me, behind her back.

I smiled.

'Shameful fellow,' he said, stroking Aisha's hair gently. 'You make my sister cry!'

'Mind your own business, lady,' I said through a smile.

Aisha released her arms from Priyank's neck and swivelled around, facing me. 'Oh, how dare you call my brother a lady?'

I rolled my eyes. 'Way did you call him here?'

'He's my brother, damn it,' she said. 'I wanted to meet him, and also' - she quickly sneaked a glance at Priyank behind her shoulder who nodded faintly - 'Priyank wants to talk to you.'

'Ha, ha, really?' I said. 'Priyanka *bhaiya* wants to talk to me.'

Aisha glared at me. 'How dare you?' she said, pointing an accusing finger at me.

I shrugged. 'I'm not interested in *her* crap,' I said. 'Do you get it?' After a pause, I added, 'alright then, I'll leave you two sisters at it.'

I walked past them out the main door with a cursory glance at both of them.

Not without a bang of the door, of course.

'What is wrong with you?' Aisha said as I entered my room a few hours later. What a match it was of *Delhi Daredevils*!

'What?' I said, fishing an ear bud from the bedside drawer.

'You insulted my brother!'

I straightened up and pricked my ears.

'He'd come down all the way from Mumbai,' she said, 'to talk some sense into you and you didn't even listen to him. If you can't respect my brother, how do you expect me to *respect your sister?'*

'No,' I said, taking a step forward, 'It's not like that. It's the other way round. Since you' - I waggled my finger at her – 'are not good to my sister, I am not good *to your brother!'*

I threw the used ear bud on the bed.

'Oh, is it?' she screamed. 'But what about all the…'

I turned a deaf ear. Honestly I didn't feel like arguing with her today.

As the yellow light of the lamp glistened past her face I noticed her ugliness shrouded her beauty. Wrinkles had formed at the edge of her eyes, dark circles nestled underneath them, black heads spotted her nose, and a hundred little pimples framed her cheeks. Or maybe I never noticed them before.

I was about to say something, but then later pursed my lips. There wasn't any point discussing it any further. If you can't be good to my family, I can't be good to yours.

I shook my head and gazed at her one last time as if to know *what is happening to us?* Sensing my silence, she fell silent. I could see a glint of sadness on her face mirrored by my own. A lone tear stood at the edge of her eyes, and I could tell from her pursed lips and clenched fists, she was trying hard not to set them free. I swallowed a huge lump in my throat and scarpered down the room toward the balcony.

Outside the weather was balmy. A light breeze rustled past the leaves of the banyan trees along the road. I lit my cigarette and exhaled a puff. Plumes of white smoke rose up and above. In the distance I saw a cluster of yellow lights from the homes across the road. The lights were a blur a moment later and then a pudgy ball of yellow. I wiped the tears that had mysteriously sprung up in my eyes. I couldn't be sure about the chilling thought that surfaced in my mind a while ago.

Was I falling out of love with her?

26. THE MUCH NEEDED BREAK
May 2011, Delhi

By the third month of our marriage, a deep chasm had formed in our relationship. I was sure whatever was to happen now, absolutely nothing would restore the old times. We might reach a consensus sometime in the future, but the void would always remain for the rest of our life.

We had stopped talking to each other completely now. I had forgotten the feel of her touch and we slept opposite to each other on the bed. She ignored all others in my family who ignored her in turn. I had immersed myself in beer and IPL. Thank God for cricket.

Some days I had long conversations with mom and Priya in their room about Aisha. Obviously it was my mistake of getting married to her, I was told. Statements like 'I would have definitely got you a better bride' or questions like 'Why were you in such a big hurry to get married?' formed the crux of our conversations. All of them invariably ended with declarations like 'see this is what happens when you don't listen to your elders'.

Quite simply, I was blamed for everything.

Honestly, I was fed up of everybody in my life, not just Aisha but my own family as well. I wanted to be out of here and spend time with myself for a few days. Perhaps take a break from the entire human race, especially women.

Maybe this entire marriage thing is a sham. We were so happy before that, where did all the love suddenly disappear? I had seen the same question in Aisha's eyes too. But then, both of us knew we'd reached too far to come back in this relationship.

Then one day in the second week of May as I entered my room precariously, I saw her big fat suitcase flung open right over our bed. She was...packing. Was she leaving me? *Forever?*

I cleared my throat. 'Aisha, are you going somewhere?' I asked, the thought crossing my mind that we hadn't spoken in the last couple of weeks.

'Yeah,' she said.

'Em...where?'

'Mumbai...few days.'

'Oh...Ok,' I swallowed. Then almost as an afterthought, I added, 'you never told me about it.'

'Yeah,' she said, 'I'm sure you'd be interested.' Her remark was motley of sarcasm and anger.

I scratched my eyebrows. 'When is the...flight?'

'Four hours later,' she said without looking up.

She was leaving *today*, and *now*?

An hour later she wheeled her suitcase across the floor producing a screeching sound against it. I sat there reading a book... pretending to read a book. Perhaps I waited for her to wish me goodbye, a perfunctory peck on the cheek...something.

She didn't even look at me as she made her way out of the room. I shrugged. *To hell with her!*

I sauntered toward the balcony and looked below. A metallic blue *Meru Cab* waited beside our house. A minute later she transferred her luggage in the back and settled in the back seat. The driver turned the ignition of the car and off they went leaving behind a gray plume of dust in the air.

I wouldn't lie by saying I missed her, because honestly, I didn't. In fact I was relieved in her absence. My room was vacant when I entered; no frown, no anger, and no cold vibes greeted me. There were no arguments, no yelling, and most importantly no one sucked my blood.

In the following week all seemed well in the world, though, she never called me. I spent long hours outside the house with friends and cousins. Nights were spent on TV and basking in the freedom of bachelorhood.

Then exactly a week after she left, my phone rang late night. That had to be her; no one calls me that late.

It was Joe Singh.

'Hey, buddy,' I answered. 'So late, I thought you were on your ship.'

'Just returned a few days back,' he said. 'Congrats for your marriage; sorry brother, couldn't make it.'

'Oh,' I shrugged. 'Never mind, so where are you these days?'

'In Mumbai, still,' he replied, 'but now in Delhi, cousin's marriage.'

Poor guy, I thought, the cousin I mean. 'So let's catch up buddy,' I said. 'It's been a long time since we met.'

'Sure, tomorrow, *Chili's*, Vasant Kunj.'

'Done.'

'You gave her gold biscuits!' Joe Singh laughed hysterically with pounding motions of the chest that shook his broad shoulders. He produced a spluttering sound and little drops of tears appeared in his eyes. His bright red turban almost blinded me. 'You've got to be kidding, man. But why biscuits, couldn't you think of a better gift?'

We sat at *Chili's*, an American restaurant on the third floor of the Ambience Mall in Vasant Kunj. Offering cheap liquor and scrumptious continental, Mediterranean and Italian dishes, it was the perfect place for a reunion. We were meeting after six months or so. I very well remembered our last meeting. Priyank…toothpaste…squeals…and loads of laughter.

At mid day, there weren't many people around, so the waiters could concentrate on us. I had told him everything, right from the day everyone agreed for our marriage to the current state of affairs. Joe Singh had left a few days before our marriage for his assignment somewhere in the Chinese waters so he wasn't aware of the development. I told him about all the excitement and action preceding our marriage and then the trauma following it. Our platonic honeymoon trip made him laugh and that's when I told him about the gold biscuits.

'Yeah, dude…biscuits,' I replied.

He waved out his hands with a confused look on his face. 'Why?'

'Alright,' I said. 'It's a good investment, why does nobody get it? Anyway, so that was the tipping point, our love began nose-diving ever since…' I trailed off, leaning back in my chair.

I held out the beer mug and took a sip. Then slowly I told him the rest of the story.

Joe Singh listened with sincerity. His eyes were fixed on mine and I could tell from his earnest expression, his mind wasn't wandering. For once it felt good to talk...really good to talk to a man. When I finished, I let out a huge sigh. I nibbled at the cheese nachos producing a crunching sound.

Joe Singh leaned forward and placed his beer mug in front. He gave me a thoughtful glance before he parted his lips. 'I think it's your fault,' he finally said after his rumination, stretching out his hand and drawing a handful of nachos. 'You haven't been supportive enough. Don't you see she just needs your love and support?'

'What are you saying?' I let out another sigh and eyed the people around me. Damn these women! I hated even looking at them now. I gulped down the beer in long, gurgling sips.

'How? Why?'

'Ronit are you blind?' he said, narrowing his eyes. 'I mean can't you see that Aisha has sacrificed so much for you. Women are very sensitive dude; they'll take all the shit from every one provided their husband is good to them. All they want is our support and constant assurance that we love them and care for them. And you, my friend' - his index finger almost touching my nose – 'have done neither of it.'

'How do you know so much about women, anyway?' I asked; the question occurring so many times in my mind. 'You don't even have a girlfriend.'

He laughed. 'Oh, you don't want to be going there,' he said, throwing out his hands playfully. 'That's for some other day. Anyway, you better settle things with Aisha. I got my butt stuffed with toothpaste so you could get married, if you remember. Damn that bastard Priyanka!'

I laughed. 'Yeah, of course, I remember that.'

Joe Singh's eyes lit. 'Wow!' he said. 'He had such soft hands, you know. His touch against my butt felt so…wonderful. I don't mind getting it done by him again.'

'Eew! I said, struck by revulsion. 'Why have you always been so infatuated by my *sala*?' I took a long sip of the beer. 'Even during our pre-sea days, you actually were ogling at his butt while applying the toothpaste. And what sort of a psycho puts a screensaver of someone's butt, and that too, of a *guy*?'

Joe Singh giggled. His moustache slithered, the long bushes of which were half drenched in beer. 'Yeah, yeah, funny isn't it? Anyway,' he said, gulping down the remaining beer in his glass, 'let's not divert and talk about his sister. She's such a lovely person, and you love her. What are you doing, man?'

No, I didn't love her. Perhaps I have never loved her; it was an infatuation if anything. She'd been gone for a week now and I didn't miss her. On the contrary I was thrilled about it. In which part of the world would that be called love?

I ordered two more beers.

'Joe Singh,' I said. 'You are my best friend. Why do we always have to be on contradicting terms with each other? A few years earlier you always dissuaded me to be away from her, and now, when I'm happy to be away from her, you tell me it's my fault and settle things with her?'

'Okay, firstly,' he said, 'stop calling me Joe Singh, just call me Joe. How many times have I *told* you that? '

I smiled.

'And, secondly,' he shook his head, 'you're a bloody idiot, that's why I always disagree with you. Now Aisha is your wife, loving her and keeping her happy is your responsibility. You think *now* I'll tell you to be away from her?'

'Maybe,' I said with a slight shrug.

He tutted. 'Oh, you donkey! Now listen...'

His rant went on for another hour until I couldn't take his insane advice anymore. He left me with a horde of tips on *how to make your woman happy* and *what not to do in a marriage.*

On my way back home, again, as always, I wondered how the hell he knew so much about women. The guy never even had a damn girlfriend!

Later that night while smoking in the balcony I couldn't escape the thought that despite Joe Singh's words, I felt happy to be away from Aisha. In fact, I dreaded her return.

It was then that the thought of a divorce first occurred to me.

27. ALRIGHT, I'M OUT OF HERE
June 2011, Delhi

Three weeks had passed and Aisha wasn't home yet. There had been no calls from her to me or my family. I didn't call her either.

It wasn't that I cared or missed her. I was just...angry with her unconcern. How could she be so callous and inconsiderate? Mom and Priya had completely lost it by then. A series of questions flooded me about her whereabouts. I was sure a huge drama awaited her arrival.

However, all said and done, I was pretty content with my life. These three weeks had to be the best three weeks in my married life. I had seen it in movies, read it in books, how elated a husband is when his wife is not around. I always thought that was sarcastic, why would a husband be happy without his wife? But now, I know, it's a one hundred percent true; life can't be more peaceful for men than when their wives are away.

Unfortunately, my happiness didn't last more than the first week of June. One afternoon, while we were having lunch, there was a loud knock on the door. I made my way to the door anticipating the maid. And there she was, the big suitcase beside her, and a faint smile playing at the corner of her lips.

'Hey,' she said, making her way in.

I nodded. 'Where have you been all this while?'

'I think I told you before leaving,' she replied curtly.

'*Beta*, where were you?' Mom called out from behind the dining table as she came in sight of her. 'It's been three weeks now.'

Aisha walked toward her and they shared a perfunctory hug. 'Mom, I was in Mumbai with my parents,' she replied, pulling back. 'I told Ronit before leaving.'

'Yeah, I know,' mom said looking at Priya, 'but no calls, no mails…nothing?'

'Sorry mom, I was really busy an-'

'So what did you think, huh,' Priya bellowed, interrupting her. 'We have nothing to do here; just wait for your arrival and hope everything is fine with you. You know how much everyone has been worried about you here.'

Aisha drew a deep breath and tucked her hair behind her ears. 'Oh really,' she said. 'And that pretty much sums up the reason why no one called.'

With that she swirled around and trotted toward our room. The three of us in the room exchanged bitter glances.

'That is no way to talk to my sister!' I said, barging into my room right after my lunch.

'Ronit, stop!' she said and turned on her heels toward me. 'Don't get me started again. You also know she was the one who instigated me.'

'But she was right,' I countered. 'You didn't even bother giving us a call.'

She huffed before walking toward me over the other side of the bed. She crossed her arms, pouted, and gazed at me.

'So did any one of *you* call to check on me, whether my flight landed or crashed, if I was dead or alive?

That dreaded devil was back. I shook my head and cradled it in my hands.

'Oh God, not again,' I grunted. 'Why did you even come back?'

I moved backward, away from her.

There was a momentary pause. 'Fine, you know what?' she yelled back. I'll leave!'

I gnashed my teeth. 'Oh, no, actually…' I took a step toward her, held her arms, and shook her violently. 'I will leave!'

With that I hauled my phone out from my jeans and dialled a number. She panted loudly by my side and I felt like slapping her at the sight of her crocodile tears.

'Hello, Sahni uncle,' I said after three rings.

Sahni uncle is the crewing manager of Nautical Marine Company, and my mother's cousin.

'Oh hello Ronit, what's up?'

'Uncle, please assign me a ship as soon as you can, I'm in urgent need of money.'

Aisha's tearful eyes popped up.

'What happened all of a sudden, is everything okay?'

'Yeah uncle, sure, everything's okay. Just tell me when I can join.'

'Hmm…let me check.'

I heard the muffled sound of flicking pages and a pattering of keyboard. I glanced at Aisha wiping her eyes and sniffing.

'Hello…um…Ronit.'

'Yeah uncle, tell me?'

'Look son,' he said slowly. 'The only vacancy I have is on a ship two days later. Other than that we have no openings in this month.'

'Fine uncle, good enough, I'll be ready in two days then.'

'But...um...there is a problem Ronit,' he said hesitantly. 'Actually this ship passes that Somalia region frequently, you never know with the pirates these days. Why do you want to take a risk? I'll give you a ship with a better run next month.'

'Oh no uncle,' I said quickly. 'That's alright, doesn't matter. Just confirm me for it; I'll see you in the office tomorrow.'

I snapped my phone before he could say something. How would he know getting stuck with Aisha is worse than being with pirates?

'Goodbye!' I howled in her face and a flood of tears stormed their way out of her eyes again.

Two days later while handing my passport and ticket to the lady behind the check-in counter at the Indira Gandhi International Airport, I came across an envelope in my back pack. I pulled it out and inside was a letter.

A letter from Aisha...

An hour later after completing the immigration and security formalities, as I slouched in the waiting lounge, I pulled out the letter. With a heavy heart, I began reading it.

Dear Ronit,

Nothing in this world has given me more pain than our time spent together in the last few months. As you leave tomorrow, I can't help but wonder what went wrong? My heart is sore with pain and I find it difficult to breathe. I wish God brandishes his magic wand at us, transporting us back to February, on our marriage day, so we could give this a fresh start. Maybe things would still be the same, maybe not.

It would be difficult to live without you in the coming months, but then perhaps, you are right. Maybe taking a break would help, as they say - distance makes the heart go fonder. But even then, I secretly wish you could cancel this trip and come back home to me, so that we could give our marriage another try, all over again...

Your wife,
Aisha.

Without second thought, I crumpled the paper, tore it till it was a cluster of a hundred small pieces, and flung it in the dustbin beside me. Forcing out the thoughts about Aisha and her damn letter, I made my way to the passage way leading to the aircraft which would take me to the port where my ship was anchored.

28. THE AFTERNOON BEFORE THE PIRATES BOARDED - 3

25th June 2011, Transiting Indian Ocean

I swallowed hard and fought the huge lump rising in my throat. I reached for the water jug on the desk toward my left and poured a glass of water. Within a minute I gulped down three glasses. I didn't realize I was that thirsty. From behind the table, the Captain's eyes were fixed on me and a faint smile bordered his lips.

'That's it, sir,' I said, placing the glass back on the desk. 'I have planned to divorce her this time when I'm back home. I'll forget everything and lead a peaceful life thereafter.'

'Ah, is it so?' he said, leaning back and interlinking his fingers across his stomach.

'Yes sir.'

He took a deep breath, and I could tell from his expression he was in deep thought.

'Okay, first things first,' he said, placing the palm of his hand under his chin. 'Do you love her?'

I pondered. The memory of the last few months flashed in my mind.

'Not anymore,' I replied firmly.

'You sure?' he lowered his head and stared at me from over

the rim of his glasses 'She was your first love, wasn't she? You think you'll forget her just like that?' He clicked his fingers in the air.

I looked down and ran my fingers over the wooden table in front. Before answering I looked up, and said, 'yes she was, and yeah I'll forget her.'

'Really,' he leaned forward, the couch squeaking beneath him. 'You know what Ronit, open your ears and listen carefully to what I'm gonna tell you now.'

I nodded.

'When you fall in love for the first time, you can never get that person out of your mind for the rest of your life. You can never do that! You might learn to love again, or move on, or find another life partner, but the memories of your first love would always remain, no matter how hard you try to get them away…' He trailed off removing his spectacles and stared at me directly through those big, brown eyes.

'Do you not see me?' he asked with a slight shake of his head. 'It's been four decades since I first fell in love with Shikha, but she's still here.' He tapped the left side of his chest with his hand. 'I haven't seen her in like…three decades but I still love her. I can *never* forget her and you know why?' He paused for a moment, but continued without waiting for a response, 'because she was my first love.'

I said nothing and put some light on his words. I shook my head at the realization.

'You know what, sir,' I said. 'Maybe you are right; maybe I'll never forget her. But those memories would not be of love, instead of anger and resentment, and maybe regret.'

He smiled. 'Oh dear, you don't know what you are talking

about.' The grin didn't leave his face. 'Of course, even after your separation you'll still love her.'

'No way, sir,' I said with a wave, shifting on my seat. 'You can't love someone forever, especially after getting married to the same person.'

'Of course, you can,' he said, frowning. 'Where did you get such false notions about life? Why is your *sms* generation so damn cynical? Am I not in love with my wife? And that's when I haven't even been with her in a long, long time.'

'Oh sir, I don't know about –'

'Okay, let's leave the love part aside,' he snapped. 'You think *you* have done your part as a husband?'

I nodded. 'Of course, what more can a woman want?'

The smile on his face returned. 'Well, you know what Ronit, I don't think so.'

I shrugged. 'And why is that?'

'Alright, look...'

The phone in his cabin rang again. He answered it. 'Hmm... okay...alright...is it a lot? Yeah, okay, we'll come.'

'Let's take this upstairs, Ronit,' he said, removing his navy blue cap from the hook on his left, and setting it neatly over his head. 'There is a bit of traffic in this area and the second officer is not too confident about it.'

'Sure sir.'

We made our way to the top most part of the ship – the navigation bridge. Fitted with tempered glass windows all around, it offered an unfettered three sixty degree view of the ocean ahead, so absolutely nothing went unnoticed.

The sun was bright and the gray clouds failed to obscure it. The sea was almost calm and the waves caught the sunlight in its arms that shone at us. There were a few ships around us, perhaps headed for the Gulf of Aden which would connect with the Red Sea that would flow into the Mediterranean Sea. However, for now, I was sure all seafarers on these ships would want to pass safely without getting hijacked by the pirates of Somalia.

As for me, I wasn't really sure.

'Alright, Ronit,' Captain said, after taking over the watch and settling on the pilot chair. 'Where was I?'

'You were telling me that I haven't been a good husband.' I frowned.

'Oh yeah, of course,' he chuckled, making the skin at the corner of his eyes crinkle. 'So the first point I would like to make is that marriage is a compromise. No more, no less. You gain some, you lose some. Now look at your wife Aisha - she left her city, left her home and family to live with you. That's the biggest sacrifice any woman can make. But you didn't value that sacrifice. Of course, any girl would have a problem adjusting in a new home with a new family. You ought to give her some time. But instead what did you do, you always fought with her.'

He narrowed his eyes at me to the size of a slit. 'Then when your family messed around with her, you *never* supported her. I'm not blaming your family if that's what you're thinking; they have their own problems, but trust me any woman wouldn't mind all that provided her husband supports her. Instead, you chose to ignore her and partied with your friends. Now what sort of a wife would accept that?'

I averted his gaze.

'Ronit, look...' He paused till his eyes met mine again. 'Before marriage you were desperate to live with her, but later when you got all that so easily, you took things for granted. You can never take love for granted, always remember that. You say you want a divorce, but when you actually get separated, you'll realize her true worth in your life. Why are you turning your back on love so soon? Give it another chance. Divorce is not the solution, trust me. We did that and I have regretted that decision every single day of my life. Getting old with the person you love is the most remarkable dream any human can achieve. I ruined mine up, but you still have a chance. This girl loves you, I'm sure you also love her. Look at the last day; she was still trying by giving you a letter. Wake up before it's too late.'

'Alright sir, stop!' I folded my hands, almost begging him. 'It's easier said than done. You don't know my problem. And if you valued love so much, then why did you divorce your wife? You were also fed up of your wife, right? It's easier to give lessons to others, but harder to implement them. And if you loved her so much, then you could have got back together with her. Why did you not do that, huh?'

Disappointment loomed over Captain's face. He looked into the distance and appeared lost in his thoughts. Then slowly, looking back at me, he said, 'I'll tell you why...'

29. CAPTAIN'S STORY - 6
1980, Nagpur

There is nothing more powerful and splendid than the feeling of being in love; more so when you are loved back by the same person; even more so when you have married that person and plan to spend the rest of your life with her.

Yes, I was the blessed one. Only a few people in this world are fortunate enough to experience love in its fullest form as me.

It had been close to a month since we moved into a rented apartment in the southern part of this city after moving out from the orphanage. Though, I must admit, we missed our pals there and the simple life of the orphanage often, however, it never lasted more than a few moments.

We had consummated our marriage on the very first night itself, exploring our naked bodies for the first time against the silver-blue light of the moon pouring over us. The rest of the night was spent wrapped in each other's arms.

In time we realized that buying a double bed had been a wrong idea. More often than not, through the night and into the morning, we found ourselves curled into one another on one side of the bed. The bed sheet on the other half remained neat and crisp, as it had been the night before.

Mornings were the best part of my day with her warm body snuggled against mine and her face tucked under my chin. And then as my eyes would open gradually to the most pleasant sight in the world, I'd be struck with a realization together with a self-realizing smile that I had to be the luckiest man in the world.

After we woke up slowly, sometimes we made love again and on other occasions, stopped ourself after foreplay. It felt good to be in control of our desires sometimes.

That's what Shikha used to say. I hated those mornings.

After our morning rituals as she made breakfast, I pondered over my options, flicking through various newspapers in search of a job. Although I had a job in a transportation company few months back, I had left it in hope of finding a full time job. Besides the money earned there was enough as long as we were in the orphanage with food and shelter looked after, but certainly insufficient to run a family. I had some savings from that job which were to last a few weeks or at the most, a month, if we lived frugally. However, we never let that bother us; we had had our share of tough days. Absolutely nothing could dishearten us, more so, as we were together.

After breakfast, we left for companies nearby in the hope of getting a job. Yes, we. I never did anything alone; rather we never did anything alone. We found it very distressing to be away for each other. So she'd accompany me for the interviews, waiting outside, while I accompanied her for various household chores like buying vegetables, milk, et cetera.

Life was going on wonderful that way. After the interview, we'd roam around the city, romanticize on the banks of the various lakes Nagpur had to offer, and reminisce our old times. Sometimes we visited the orphanage, met our friends, our teachers, and had long chats into the evenings. Other days we'd watch new released movies, sometimes explored Nagpur's restaurants, and had long walks with our fingers interlinked against each other before returning home. Shikha would go on bantering about our old times and I would just listen to her and enjoy the lilt of her voice. At times I would hardly listen and thank God for the wonderful partner I was blessed with.

Then a few weeks later, I could sense a shade of panic in our home. We'd been married for more than a month which also meant I was jobless for that long. I didn't possess any high educational qualifications, but then, I never looked for any high brow jobs either. All I wanted was a decent job which would take care of our finances. Alongside, I had enrolled for a correspondence course from the Nagpur University, and I hadn't forgotten the promise I made to Baba.

Thankfully, two weeks later I got a job in a packaging company. The salary was modest but sufficient. But with the job came a niggling thought that we'd never anticipated. We *had* to be away from each other for more than ten hours in a day. Now that wasn't easy as since the time we'd known each other, we'd never been away for that long.

The following Monday Shikha was cooking breakfast, and the delicious aroma of *aloo paranthas* wafted toward our room. I was getting ready for the first day at work and followed the aroma from the kitchen and held Shikha from behind, my arms tight around her belly. Her trembling shoulders and rapid breathing made my throat tighten instinctively, hit by the sudden realization. She was crying. I hauled her over to face me. Her eyes were red and swollen, and it appeared she'd been crying for some time.

'Oh, Shikha,' I sighed. 'You're crying? Why?'

I cupped her face in my hands and tilted it upward toward me.

It took a minute for her to answer. 'Because you're leaving for your job,' she replied. Her voice was a squeal. 'What will I do alone till the evening,' she added sadly.

'Aw Shikha, come on.' I leaned forward and kissed her forehead. 'Don't be silly, I'll be back by evening. Then we'll go out, have dinner, and take a long walk...' I wiped her tears slowly. 'It'll be fun,' I added breathily.

'Yeah.' A wave of smile swept past her face as she sniffed. 'I'm so crazy, I love you so much.' She wrapped her arms so tight behind me, I almost gasped for breath. 'I'll wait for you in the evening.'

I kissed the top of her head softly and rested it under my chin. We retracted slowly and gazed at each other for what seemed like an hour.

After the scrumptious breakfast, we hugged one last time before I left for work.

While climbing down the stairs I wiped the little tear that had found its way out from my eyes. I smiled at a thought that occurred to me a while ago.

More than a decade and we were still to have a fight.

30. CAPTAIN'S STORY - 7
1981, Nagpur

A month had passed in my job and today was the moment of utter joy. I was handed over my first cheque for the last month. I already knew what my first buy would be.

A bouquet of flowers!

There is an unimaginable affinity between women and flowers. I learnt it on the very first day when I gifted Shikha a rose at the age of thirteen and realized it every single time thereafter. After I returned from the first day of my work, sensing her gloomy mood back home, I greeted her with a bunch of flowers. The disappointment vanished instantly from her face giving way to a full and unfettered smile and she leaped in joy and hugged me. Nothing in this world would have made her happier.

Since then to bask in that wonderful smile, I found myself going home regularly with flowers. Even hours later or on the bed at night, she'd remember about it, giggling to herself, and thank me for that gesture as if I'd done a huge thing. It's not too hard to keep a woman happy, I realized. All they want is our love, care, support and apparently a good ear.

Life is simple indeed, if we don't complicate it. Often it's the smallest of things that fill our heart with joy. For her it was the flowers, for me it was her smile.

Today on my way back home I bought a big bouquet of flowers with red and white roses around the border, assorted bunch of fuchsia, red and pink lilies, tulips and violets at the centre with carnations sprinkled liberally over them. In my other hand was a small packet of chocolates.

As I clambered up the stairs for my flat, I heard familiar voices whooping out toward the corridor. I knocked the door to our flat. At the sight of flowers, Shikha's hand flew to her mouth, and her eyes widened. She embraced me and we kissed softly.

'Look who's here!' she squealed in joy, stepping aside.

I entered and was ecstatic at the sight of Rajiv and Swati – our best friends from the orphanage – staring excitedly at me from across the room. I leaped toward them and we hugged.

'Wow, guys!' I shrieked. 'What a nice surprise, how *are* you guys?'

We retracted slowly. Rajiv and I held each other's arms, and then hugged once more. Rajiv was looking good as ever in his suede jacket and jeans, and I always found Swati a very pleasing person. She was wearing an auburn coloured suit that highlighted her supple figure.

'All good, buddy!' he exclaimed. 'All good!'

'Yeah,' Swati said. She turned toward Shikha and winked. 'Actually better than good, we came over to share some good news with you two.'

'Tell me then.' I waved out my hands at them. 'I'm all ears.'

We settled down in our seats and I saw their eyes light up. There was a hushed silence in the room and they shared furtive glances, throwing *guess what* looks at me.

'What?' I said impatiently. 'What are you people hiding?'

'They're getting married!' Shikha announced, hopping on her seat.

'What?' I bought my hands together. 'Wow!' I cried. 'When and how did this all happen?'

'Okay, Okay,' Rajiv said. 'Let me answer your questions, one by one.'

He leaned back; crossed his legs over, and spoke with a twinkle in his eyes.

'As for your *what* – yes, you heard it right - Swati and I are getting married. As for your *when* – well, I guess - the day you guys' - he threw his finger at me and Shikha – 'got married and now the more important *how* of your question.' He slipped his arm over Swati's shoulder. 'The reason is pretty much *you* guys, my friend.'

'We?' I scrunched up my face, glancing blankly at him and Swati and then turned my gaze toward Shikha. 'How's that?'

'Yeah Shekhar, you guys,' Swati said as she rose up and walked toward Shikha. She patted her arms and smiled. 'You guys have inspired us all at the orphanage – to live, to love, and to embrace life. You have set the example for us that all one needs to be happy and content in life is true love and companionship. In fact, it's not just the two of us who plan to tie the knot; you have showed the way to many others at the orphanage. Thank you from all of us.'

I cocked my head gleefully toward Shikha. She appeared completely enamoured by Swati's words.

'Thanks,' I acknowledged. 'That was really sweet, good to know that *we* inspired you, and well, others.' I turned my gaze at Rajiv. 'Wow!' I said, shaking my head, still absorbing the *inspiration* part. 'So when is the date?'

'Pretty soon, brother,' he replied with a wink. 'Pretty soon.'

We chatted late into the evening about our childhood days, our time at the orphanage and how blessed we'd been to be a part of it. Rajiv teased me and Shikha reminded us how he teased her over her ponytail and the day he broke my teeth. How much we used to hate him then. Funny, how time changes everything.

Before bidding goodbye, we hugged each other profusely, and promised to attend their wedding. When they left, Shikha banged the door shut and leaped at me like a monkey.

'Wow!' she screamed; her hands over her cheeks. 'You got me such lovely flowers!'

31. CAPTAIN'S STORY - 8
1981, Nagpur

Why do people not love freely? And why do they not value the special moments as life passes by?

I pondered over these questions while I watched Shikha gorge on the chocolate ice cream. We sat in her favourite restaurant not too far from our place. We had watched a movie before lunch, and now, after she'd be done digging on her ice cream, I had the tickets ready for our second movie of the day. For the rest of the evening, we planned to stroll by the banks of Futula Lake and witness the waning light of the sun on completion of its shift in this part of the world.

And then a little gift would await Shikha's arrival in the evening at our home.

Today was our first quarterly wedding anniversary.

Both of us found the idea of celebrating wedding anniversaries every year a very boring concept. Special moments like these should be celebrated more often. By definition, of course, it's the annual observation of a past event, we knew that. However, we never wanted to wait one full year to cherish the most important day of our life. So we'd decided on celebrating it quarterly. I wanted it monthly, though I knew that would be taking things too far.

Coming back to my questions, I guess, I had been fortunate to be blessed with Shikha's love. Loving her is so easy, so natural; I presume she would have made the perfect life partner to almost anyone in this world. And for the second question, well, each and every moment spent with her is so many lifetimes of happiness put together. Who would not value those moments after all?

I leaned back in my chair and observed her. Her eyes were fixed below, on her ice cream, and absolutely nothing could budge her. I fondly remembered the past three months of our marriage. Each and every day had been memorable, with each passing day better than the previous one.

After she was done with the ice cream, her lips were smeared with its brownish remnants. She whisked her tongue over it playfully and finally tilted her head toward me. Her eyes had the look of a desire half-fulfilled, so I ordered another one.

'No,' she said only half-heartedly, 'I'm done.'

'Sure you are,' I teased. I clicked in the air in the waiter's direction, 'One more!'

I checked the time in the watch on my left arm. We still had over an hour for the movie.

And then, I watched her again as her next round of ice cream arrived.

Several hours later, as we walked with our hands together over the last stretch of road that led to our home, my stomach gurgled. A tingling sensation ran through my body in the anticipation of giving her the little present that awaited her and watching her loving reaction.

I had summoned Rajiv's help and handed him the duplicate key to our apartment to help me with the little surprise. It was nothing fancy though, just a gentle reminder how much I loved her and what she meant to me. There was nothing better in this world than the feeling of having her surprised.

'Wow!' she squealed in delight when the door to our apartment creaked open. 'This is so beautiful.' Her hands were over her face.

She was staring at our front wall that was adorned with red roses. They were arranged to form the following words: 'Happy first quarterly anniversary Shikha, Love you forever'. The word 'love' was in shape of a heart - actually three concentric hearts – with red roses at the centre followed by white and pink roses outlining them.

She leaned on me, hugging me tightly, almost squeezing me. I led her towards our room where a few gifts neatly gift wrapped and tied ribbons peeked at her. Her eye balls popped out and hands flew back again to her face.

'Thanks,' she said and neatly undid the cello-tape from the gifts.

'Wow, this is a beautiful sari…and, oh my God' - she thrust her hand over her heart – 'nice sandals.'

'This is a great perfume,' she added in gaiety after opening the third one, spraying a little over herself.

'Wow! This is so good,' she said for the fourth time.

A little further up, on the chest of the drawers, sat a letter which I wrote in the last few nights. I'd slip out of bed when she'd be deep in her sleep, carefully freeing my arms from her own.

Her eyes fell on it and the eyed me sceptically. 'What's that?'

She rose from the bed and with a faint smile and raised eyebrows headed for the letter. My heart thumped when she ran her fingers through the words on the envelope – 'For my beautiful wife!' it said.

Very slowly she slid the letter out as if to enjoy every moment of it.

And then, she began reading it.

My dear Shikha,

From where do I even begin? More than a decade has passed, and yet, it feels as if I fell in love with you only today. The spark and passion hasn't receded, if anything, it's only grown by leaps and bounds, with each passing day.

What would I ever do without you? I often wonder and fail miserably to answer my question that rings occasionally in my mind. I would rather be dead, comes the only sane answer. But then, that's not the way our love is supposed to end, my love. We're gonna live, and grow old with each other, and die in each other's arms, perhaps half a century later...

A very, very happy quarterly anniversary, my dear, and here's for hoping many, many, and many more to come.

With all my love, and then a little more,

Your loving husband, Shekhar.

'Aw Shekhar,' she pressed the letter to her heart. 'This is so beautiful, I love you so much.'

She opened her arms toward me, and happily, I found myself reaching for them.

'Actually...um,' she muttered under her breath. 'There's a little present I'd like to give you as well.'

We retracted slowly, and then, when she told me she was pregnant, I knew her gift was far, far better than mine.

32. CAPTAIN'S STORY – 9
1981, Nagpur

Over the next few weeks, our happiness knew no bounds. We were on cloud nine as we were having a new member in our home. It felt all the more wonderful as for many years it was just the two of us.

A week after the revelation, we visited the orphanage to seek the blessings of our elders. They were all thrilled about the news and showered us with their guidance and a deluge of advice. They felt we were too young to parent a child. We never felt likewise; although, young, our maturity was at least a decade ahead of our age. Nevertheless, we had a great time there and it felt wonderful to share the news with them. The atmosphere was such as if everyone was having a child.

Back home, I'd ensured Shikha didn't indulge in any physical activity or work. I was assisting her in the kitchen and various household chores as much as I could, after my office hours. Not that I didn't help her before, but after reading a load of self-help books about pregnancy, we'd become paranoid. Sure they helped, but they drove us crazy. Nine months felt like an eternity.

At night, before falling asleep, we'd ponder over the name of our child. We thought about various names, both male and female, of course. We also anticipated the prospect of having twins, triplets, quadruplets...

I told you, we were getting paranoid.

A few days later, we realized it wasn't an easy task. Both of us had to be agree to it, and more often than not, it wasn't the case. What she liked, I didn't, and vice versa. However, just the discussion of names brought us tremendous joy.

Those days, I felt more in love with her than ever before. After all, she was the one fulfilling my eternal dream of having a family. We loved more; we kissed more, and awaited the arrival of our long-cherished dream. And then, we planned to take that dream of five kids, right after this one.

In the first month itself the pace of time had slowed down considerably, and in the workplace, it moved at a snail's pace. When I returned home, I'd reach out for her belly, running my hands over it, in anticipation of that elusive bump. Of course, I'd be disappointed. May be we *were* too immature for just a month had passed.

Shikha was even ahead of me in this regard. She'd already begun shopping – clothes, toys, and whatever baby stuff she could lay her hands on. It did burn a huge hole in my pocket, but then again, I'd loved that myself. In fact, I accompanied her on those shopping sprees.

We'd begun controlling our expenses too – no more movies, no outside meals, and whatever extra we splurged on. Of course, the flowers never stopped. The money we saved, howsoever paltry, was set aside.

That super-excited and super-exhilarated state continued for the next month, until one day, I found an envelope in the bedside drawer while searching for some papers. My body froze at the sight of it. On the ivory colour of the envelope, following words were printed in red ink:

'SURYA ABORTION CLINIC'

33. CAPTAIN'S STORY – 10
1981, Nagpur

'What is this Shikha?' I flung the envelope on her lap. She was sipping tea on the wooden chair in the balcony. I did realize that had to be the first time I'd raised my voice at her.

'Shikha!' I was louder this time over her complete nonchalance. 'I'm asking you something.'

'What?' she said, turning her face toward me, 'Can't you see it? I got an abortion done Shekhar, what else?'

I was taken aback. 'But why?'

I shook her chair. At that, some tea spilled from the cup on to her legs.

'Aw!' she hopped out of the chair. 'It's scalding!' She cradled her legs to assuage the pain. 'What are you doing? What's wrong with you?'

'What's wrong with *me*?' I picked up the envelope from the floor and slammed on her face. 'What's wrong with *you* Shikha? Who gave you the right to get this done?'

She rose from the chair and looked ahead in the distance ignoring me and my question. I followed her gaze. There wasn't anything remotely important in comparison to what I was asking. The streets were lined with dirt and garbage with a few vehicles running past, the trees on the side of the road rustled in the wind, and a few children played on the muddy ground to our right.

A minute later, when she continued ignoring me, I took a step forward and pulled her close to face me. 'At least tell me, Shikha.' I was softer this time. 'What happened? Why did you do this?'

She took a slow breath. 'Can't you see it, Shekhar,' she said in a tone that demanded sympathy. 'The amount of sacrifices we've started making already even before the child is born. Imagine what would happen after that. You've stopped taking me out for dinner or movies; there are hardly any presents or surprises from you anymore. I don't want a life where we are struggling do get even the basic needs, and of course, with a child, things would get worse.'

I released her arms violently and she stumbled on her feet. 'But why didn't you bother discussing it with me first.'

She maintained her poker-face. I glared at her, expecting a justified reasoning. But she didn't even budge, continued looking in the distance.

'At least say something, Shikha.'

'Come on Shekhar,' she said, avoiding my gaze, looking at the children in the ground. 'You know if I had discussed it with you, you would have never allowed me to take this step. That time this is what felt right to me and so I went ahead with it. And besides' - she swirled over and looked in my eyes – 'it was growing inside me; I don't need to take anybody's permission to get rid of it, Shekhar.'

With that, she stormed inside, leaving me alone with tears and a gnawing question.

Was that our first fight?

34. CAPTAIN'S STORY – 11
1981, Nagpur

The next few days the world felt a different place altogether. She seemed confused and irritated as though I was responsible for the abortion. We weren't speaking much to each other and our eyes barely met. However whenever they did connect, I wanted to ask her the same question over and over again.

Why did you get the damn abortion?

I wasn't sure I was satisfied with the answer she had given me a few days back. I knew we'd stopped splurging on inconsequential activities, all those movies and outings, but then she'd suggested that to me. And if she hated it that much, why didn't she ever tell me before?

The more I thought, the more confused I became. But soon, I realized that money *had* to be the reason. Perhaps, she never wanted to embarrass me by being open of my ineptitude to earn enough money.

I tried forgetting about the incident. We were still young and could pursue our family dream, even later, when we were well off. But even if I'd tried, I couldn't avoid a divide slowly forming in our relationship.

The week following the abortion, I thought of befriending her again. I loved her madly and never wanted anything to come between us. We'd not spoken amiably since the day of our first fight and it felt a lifetime without her words. When I returned home in the evenings, she'd open the door for me with a cold look in her eyes. We didn't kiss, we didn't hug as before. We had dinner quietly and after washing the dishes, she'd slip into the bed, her back toward me. On the other side of the bed, I'd hope for sleep to take over my soul and transport me into another world for the next eight hours, away from the sad realization of what my life had become.

Once in a while, I tried striking a conversation with her, but they were often stilted, evoking only sighs and nods from her. I kept looking at her in anticipation of something, but was always disappointed. She had a permanent look of despondency on her face, and I was sure now she felt as bad as me about the adoption.

Slowly, I took responsibility of all that had transpired in the past few days. As a man of the house, if you're not earning enough to support your family, you have to be man enough to at least accept that. I brought myself to the conclusion that perhaps she meant well as there wasn't another option. In just about two weeks, I had already forgiven her in my mind. That was, after all, the maximum I could have been mad at her.

Meanwhile, my attempts at winning her back weren't helping. Then one day, more than three weeks after the abortion, I'd made up my mind of sorting things out with her. I planned to apologize to her for everything, from not earning enough to start a family to not being supportive with her decision, and more importantly for raising my voice at her, something I felt miserable about ever since that day. My heart thudded hard in my chest every time at the thought of it. *How could I even do that?*

I slowly walked up to the kitchen. She was chopping vegetables, her back towards me. I could feel the blood rushing to my cheeks in anticipation of her reaction. However my heart told me she'd forgive me and then I planned to love her more, be more caring and supportive, and forget about family planning until I was capable of it.

I cleared my throat. 'Shikha,' I called out as softly as I could.

'Hmm…'

'Em, I was wondering…' I said, closing the distance between us. '…can't we forget what happened and start all over again.'

She stopped moving her hands and kept the knife aside. After a quick glance at me behind her shoulder, she took a deep breath and turned toward me.

'Look Shekhar,' she said, her eyebrows arched and face curled in a deep frown. 'I'm deeply hurt by what I did and in case you *still* do not realize the reason of my abortion, it's you. You don't earn enough even for the two of us, let alone our child. In the last two months in order to save money, we've been cutting costs everywhere. I can't buy anything for myself or for the house and that's when the child is not even born. How would we even survive after that?'

'So what do you want Shikha?' I asked politely. 'You know I'm trying, at least give me some time.'

'Yeah, well,' she sighed. 'That's all you can do, just t-r-y.'

She turned over with a shake of her head and continued chopping the vegetables.

'Come on, Shikha,' I protested, pressing my arm against her shoulder. 'You know I'm trying hard, one day I'll get where you want me to be.'

'Yeah, right, one day,' she said, not trying to hide the sarcasm from her words.

I retracted back my arm. A little phase of silence fell between us. I contemplated what she said. Was I such a big loser? My own wife thinks that way. My Shikha thinks that way, *my Shikha...*

'Shikha,' I said, ignoring my thoughts. 'I promise I'll give you all the comforts of life some day, just give me time. Don't turn your back at me like that, please don't do that.'

'Shekhar, come on.' Her face was contorted when she turned around again. 'We both know that day will never come, let's not fool ourselves.'

'Why are you saying that?' I said, holding both her arms. 'Don't you trust me? And when did money become so important anyway. God, why are we even having this discussion? Do you not love me anymore?'

'Of course money is important,' she said, widening her eyes. 'We're not kids anymore, Shekhar, living in that orphanage. We're adults now. Please be reasonable. We cannot survive with love alone; we need to be practical now.'

'Alright Shikha,' I said, tightening my grip on her arms. 'I understand what you're saying. I had promised Baba and I'm promising you, we *will* become well-off someday soon.'

'Oh God,' she cringed. 'Don't even get your Baba in all this, what did he do, huh? All his life he tried and tried, but eventually died a poor man. Even your fate would be the same.' She let go off my hands and wagged her finger menacingly at me.

'You're just a loser like him, after all.'

35. CAPTAIN'S STORY – 12
1981, Nagpur

When did money become more important than love?

As I slowly sipped my whiskey, the following evening, I grappled with the question ruffling my mind. I sat on the balcony and couldn't stop the damned tears leaking out from my eyes. I didn't want Shikha to see them, she was inside, somewhere, or perhaps outside, I didn't notice. My heart welled with anger as much as I tried to forget what she had said yesterday.

You're just a loser like him after all...

Why Baba? I rolled the glass churning the yellow liquid inside and then gulped it down in one sip. I hated its taste, but my colleagues - *losers like me* - in my workplace told me it makes you forget what you want to forget. So, yeah, what the heck?

I had never imagined I could ever be so angry with Shikha. She shouldn't have said that those words, she should never have...I poured some more whiskey in the glass and topped it up with soda.

Behind me, I heard a woman rant. 'Yes, now, that'll make you rich!'

I turned round and Shikha was staring down at me in repugnance. I clenched my fingers around the glass and my lower lip trembled. My head wobbled and in a fit of a rage I hurled the glass few inches away from her evoking a loud, clattering noise when it hit the wall beside her. She recoiled away from it.

'Shut up! And get the hell out of here!' I roared.

And then I passed out.

When I awoke, the sun had already set and given way to the moon. It hung low in the cloudless sky, offering plumes of white to the ebony backdrop. Crickets chattered close by and the birds had begun their evening trill. I rose to me feet slowly, feeling the piercing pain in my head, and plunked down on the bed in our room.

A few days passed this way in an alcoholic haze. I was still not able to get rid of her bitter taunt and was mad at her for denigrating my father. He wasn't a loser. If anything, he was a man of stout character and perseverance. He sacrificed all his comforts of life for mine. In fact, he even gave place to her and her father when they needed it most.

And now she thinks he was a loser.

Everything is money, I decided those days, the biggest virtue of humans. Love, compassion, affection only follows it. My own wife taught me that, someone whom I thought would be the last person in the world who'd think that way. But then, I have myself to blame. That's what happens when you love someone more than life itself...*more than yourself,* you blur the reality and live in a world of fantasy.

Things were changing now. Slowly, but steadily, we were drifting apart, more so in my mind. This time I never felt of sorting things with her. I was deeply hurt by her callousness and complete disregard to my feelings. I constrained myself in my own world of thoughts and alcohol. She too, never bothered, by the way

The following weeks it got even worse. On most of the days, she'd stopped cooking for me feigning a headache or fever. I'd return tired from the office only to find her sleeping or resting on the couch.

'Did you cook anything today,' I asked her one Friday evening. 'I'm starving.'

She was cradling her temples and her eyes were shut. At my presence, she scrunched up her face as if she was in deep pain. 'No, I'm not feeling well today.'

'Shikha!' I said irately. 'Cut the crap OK, this is the fifth straight day you haven't cooked anything. Stop giving me that pained expression, always. I can't be looking after my work and your work at the same time. I am tired when I return and need some food before I sleep. What did you do all day today apart from lying there?'

She perked up and glared at me. 'So you married me to have your food cooked and have someone to look after your house, is it? Why didn't you get a maid in that case who could do all that for you?'

Funnily enough, her pain seemed to vanish while she spoke those words.

I shook my head. 'Just go to hell!' I yelled before marching to my room.

Arguments like these that our home had never seen hitherto became a routine paradigm. We often fought, seldom spoke, and never shared a cozy moment. Maybe all that hogwash they say about wife and marriage is true. There can be no such term as a happy married man. If there was, then his wife would be dead.

In the days that followed, I wouldn't say I tried improving our relationship, but yet, I never faltered in my duties. I still worked and, dutifully, at the end of the month handed over my entire salary to her, of course, after separating my share for the alcohol. The thought of cheating on her never occurred in mind and I remained loyal as ever. There were days when I cooked for her and yet other days when I got the groceries and other stuff for the house after her continued pretence of headache or body ache or fever or whatever.

I learnt staying silent maintained peace and harmony in our home. On days I opened my mouth, she opened it wider and bigger, until we'd yell our lungs out at each other after which she'd sob in one corner and I'd drink in the other. There was a spectacular satisfaction achieved in watching those tears roll down her cheeks.

After all she'd been the one who made them appear in my eyes in the first place.

36. CAPTAIN'S STORY – 13
1981, Nagpur

'Why the hell did you not tell me about Rajiv and Swati's wedding?' I stomped into our flat right after work one day and yelled out.

Close to two months had passed after the revelation of her abortion and we were still not on talking terms, if yelling and screaming at each other doesn't qualify, that is to say. She held a gloomy face all day as if I was responsible for everything. When she was around with that sullen look and weary eyes, it felt that I had to be the worst husband ever as if I'd been inflicting a case of domestic violence on her. I ignored her outright and engulfed myself in alcohol.

But then today, I couldn't keep the anger to myself. Rajiv had showed up at my workplace and admonished me for not making it to his wedding. He said Swati had personally handed over their wedding card to Shikha and exhorted us to be a part of it. A distant relative of her had organized the wedding in a banquet hall and naturally they were excited about it. It was a far cry from our wedding in that shady district court.

And Shikha never even told me about it. Obviously, she couldn't attend the wedding alone and perhaps she'd be embarrassed in the company of a *loser*.

She sat on the bed and casually read a magazine.

'*Shikha!*' The blood in my veins boiled. 'I'm asking you something, will you stop ignoring me like that.'

She looked up, away from me, ran a finger on her temple and appeared lost in thoughts.

'Of course, I told you,' she replied finally, her eyes settling back on the magazine.

'At least look at me when you lie,' I said, moving closer. 'God damn it!'

'I'm not lying, I did tell you,' she repeated her lie with the same fervour.

'No, you didn't, you liar,' I snapped. 'Why would you even lie about that? Are you ashamed of even going out with me now? They are our friends; that's the least we could've done for them. Or now, you consider even them *losers* because' - I held out my hands and made quotation marks with my fingers – '*they are poor like me.*'

'OK, fine!' she said, rolling her eyes. 'If that's what you want to think, go ahead, I don't care. But I thought I told you.' She ran a languid hand through her hair.

'Oh yeah, right, now you *thought* you told me,' I said before storming out the room.

The following evening in my drinking session, I decided to make up for our absence at their wedding. The least we could've done is getting them a nice present. After my drink, I headed toward Shikha and braced myself for another taxing conversation.

I asked her for some money and my intention of a gift. It's weird, I thought, to be asking for money from her and justify its need when I did all the hard work.

'I don't have any,' she muttered under her breath.

'But I just gave you few days back,' I squealed in anger, 'my entire salary!'

'You did?' She raised her eyebrow at me. 'When? I don't remember.'

'Oh God!' I clenched my fists. 'What's wrong with you? Last Tuesday…I think.'

She had a faraway look in her eyes. I waited for her to respond.

'Sorry,' she finally spoke with an air of indifference, 'but I think now *you* are lying. You spend way too much money on your alcohol, you didn't give me anything.'

With that she brazed past me toward the living room.

'Close the door,' she said. 'I'm going for a walk.'

I could see what she was doing, irritating me on purpose. *But why?* What's wrong with her? Am I such a bad husband, just because I don't earn enough? She doesn't tell me about my best friend's wedding so she doesn't need to be with me and get embarrassed; she doesn't talk to me, ignores my presence, blows whatever little I earn, and pretends I'm a fool who would believe her lame excuse of not remembering.

We shouldn't have married; I came to the conclusion few days later. Perhaps marriage torpedoes the love between humans. And that's exactly what happened in our case.

Then two days later came the day of our second quarterly anniversary. I laughed at the thought of it. We spent the entire day *away* from each other. I wasn't sure if she even remembered it and couldn't care any less.

That night a thought occurred to me. *Who knows this might just be our last quarterly anniversary?*

Then later, I kicked myself for entertaining such a negative thought. Of course, things would get better, I hoped.

37. CAPTAIN'S STORY – 14
1981, Nagpur

It is heartbreaking to think that the enormous love you once had for your wife was diminishing. As much as I tried, I couldn't stop myself from feeling distraught about our situation.

I'm not sure if I could say that I still loved her, but even then, I couldn't bring myself to the affirmation that I didn't love her either. There was still a corner in my heart that wept for her, everyday. Should I give our relation another chance?

Perhaps we'd come too far in our marriage for any hopes of rapprochement, or perhaps, not. We'd loved each other close to a decade until we got married; this is certainly not the way this was supposed to end.

OK, then!

I got up from the couch. I'll give us one last shot.

'But what happened?' Rajiv said, curiosity manifest in his eyes. 'You guys were madly in love.'

I had ordered a cup of coffee and Rajiv ordered tea. We sat in a small *dhaba* near my workplace during our lunch break. I couldn't handle the confusion alone and Rajiv was my best bet for it. As I looked up at him, I could see his eyes staring back at me in concern. Obviously, neither he nor Swati had even an inkling of our messed up relationship.

'Yeah, Rajiv,' I said, disappointment lurking loud and clear in my voice. 'That's what marriage does to you, suddenly responsibility and money becomes more important than love.'

'Huh!' He crossed his arms around his chest. 'Really?'

'Yes, my friend,' I said, nodding. 'She even got our child aborted for that reason.'

'*What?*' The cup almost fell from his hand. He banged it on the saucer and leaned forward in his chair. 'But why? You guys were so excited about it.'

'Yeah, I know,' I said, offering a faint smile that faded as quickly as it had turned up. 'I thought that too, but for Shikha, apparently, money was the concern.' I shook my head and sipped my coffee. 'She said I don't earn enough to have a family,' I added dejectedly.

'That's ridiculous,' he said with an air of finality. 'When did money come between you guys?'

'Exactly,' I said, 'that's what I told her. Wonder when that became so important to her.'

'Oh God!' he said and threw his right leg on the other. 'So much has happened and you are telling me this *now*, wonder how Swati would react to all this. Shikha hasn't mentioned a word about this to her.' He narrowed his eyes and thought for a while. 'Yeah, she hasn't, else she'd have told me, surely.'

'How would she tell her?' I said. 'She is embarrassed to have me as her husband as I'm a labourer, earning peanuts. I'm just not good enough for her now. And you know why we didn't turn up for your wedding?' I asked him but then continued without expecting an answer. 'She didn't even *tell* me about it, maybe she's embarrassed even in my company.'

Rajiv's face crinkled in disagreement. 'No, that can't be true, why would you say that?'

'So why else do you think, huh?' I asked firmly, ordering another coffee.

He let out a sigh and brought his hand to his chin, twiddling his finger around it. He glanced at me from across the table and then turned his gaze away. I could see he was thinking... *but what?*

'I don't think,' he spoke finally after his rumination, 'that you guys should give up on each other so soon.'

'So then, please, tell me what should I do?'

'OK, here's the thing...'

We sat there for two more hours and he managed convincing me that all is not lost. He told me that I don't need any advice on love and it wouldn't be too difficult for a romantic like me to rekindle our relationship. Actually, I told him, I thought likewise. I promised him I'll talk it out with Shikha and address our issues instead of ignoring them. He also exhorted me to give up alcohol and once again I said, I will.

The same evening, I sat on my bed and wondered how to break the ice with her. She was in another room as lately even our presence in the same room gnawed at us. I perked myself up and marched into her room. As usual a gloomy face greeted me.

'Listen um...Shikha,' I shifted from one foot to the other. 'We need to talk.'

'Yeah,' she croaked and rose toward a cabinet on her left. She pulled out a paper from a drawer and walked toward me.

'Here,' she said handing it to me.

'What's this?' I asked curiously, slowly opening the paper. My jaw dropped at the sight of it. 'What? You want a divorce?'

She nodded slowly. 'Yes.'

My body froze. I couldn't stop my hands from trembling. Inside my heart sprang into action and banged loudly against my chest. I read the letter, re-read it, and then one last time. The initial feeling of distress gave way to anger and I scrunched up the paper in a ball and threw on her face.

'You bitch, what do you think of yourself?'

'Shekhar,' she said firmly. 'I don't want to have any argument here, just sign the papers and leave me alone.'

I took a step closer and launched myself at her, slapping her once, twice, and then a third time.

'Why? Are you having an affair with someone?'

She stood motionless but her eyes, those eyes, *the way they panicked; it was…as if…*

A chilling sensation ran through my body and the hairs on the back of my neck stood up.

'Oh my God! You are having an *affair?*' Suddenly my breathing grew heavier. 'You are having an affair, aren't you?' I thumped my forehead with my arms. Tears gushed out from my eyes. 'Since…since when?'

'That's…none of your business, Shekhar,' she sobbed, cradling her face in her hands. 'Please, please sign the papers and go.'

'Of course, I will!' I ran one hand to wipe away the tears of my eyes and gathered the paper with the other. 'You know…' I said, struggling to draw out words through my choked throat,

'...I blamed myself for everything, and today, I thought I would resolve our issues, but...you gave me this. I loved you so much and you were...having an *affair* all this while.'

Without further ado I signed the papers and threw them back on her face.

'Here,' I sniffled. 'Enjoy yourself. I'm out of here and never want to see your face again.'

Amidst high-pitched wails of Shikha, I packed my luggage, washed my face, and stormed out the house.

Next morning, I boarded a train to Mumbai and never returned to Nagpur.

38. TODAY, 25ᵀᴴ JUNE 2011
Transiting Indian Ocean

'And then what happened?' I have never been so intrigued with someone else's story. And that too, a love story of a fifty year old man.

I glance at our Captain. Tears well up in his eyes and he finds it difficult to speak. He doesn't reply and there is a morose look on his face. I notice a gentle quiver in his stance, and I understand. He hasn't completed his story and tells me that the worse is still to come. *What can be worse?* I wonder. I mean getting a divorce from your childhood sweetheart just few months after marriage is tragic enough.

Pensively he looks ahead from our steaming ship *Adriatic Wave* toward a sight that is quintessential of a beautiful evening. The moon is full and over a million stars gleam from above us, shining and lending their luminosity to the late evening sky which is predominantly clear. The dark grey water below bathes in the ivory hue of the moon. There is a light breeze which adds to the serenity of the Indian Ocean.

'Ronit, do you see something ahead on the horizon, perhaps fine on the starboard bow,' Captain asks me, wiping his moist eyes, 'A boat maybe?' A stark hollowness has understandably crept in his voice.

I pick up the binoculars and adjust my vision through them. Frankly I am so much caught up in his story that I am hardly interested.

'No, sir,' I reply nonchalantly, 'Probably a low altitude star.' I was hardly looking.

I want to know more, dwell deeper into his heart. I want to know why even after the divorce with his wife some three decades ago, he is still madly in love with her?

I presume he is crazy, like all other ship Captains are, particularly at the age of fifty. After spending more than half of their life at sea, all these guys are left with is poignant thoughts. I mean how else can one love someone forever?

And he hasn't even seen her in the past thirty years.

A few minutes later, the pirates boarded...

PART ~ 3

39. SO WHAT HAPPENED THEN?
August 2011, Somewhere in Somalia

So then why do you still love her?
I've been meaning to ask him this question since the last two months and have failed miserably at it. *And where the hell is your mistake?*

The Captain is sitting towards my left on the far side of the bridge, his head propped against the bulkhead. There are more than ten members of the crew between us and there is no way he can tell me the answers, if at all I am able to ask those questions, that is to say.

He told me that afternoon – before the pirates boarded, close to two months back - that it was entirely his fault; he couldn't understand his wife after their marriage. I'm not sure if I'll ever agree with that. That *bitch* got the abortion done, that *bitch* maligned his father and then the Captain for not earning enough, that *bitch* wanted the divorce, not him, and the worst of all – she had an extra marital *affair?* With so much love around, how *could* she?

Instead of hating her, he...*loves her? Three decades after their divorce...?*

I draw an audible breath. Apart from struggling with these questions, I can't come to terms with *what happened to my own life?* As much as I hate Aisha, I can't bring myself to the acquiescence that I would divorce her. Of course, not even a shred of doubt exists in my mind about it, but still it's…sad is probably the closest I can get in describing it.

And as if that isn't pitiable enough, the pirates have made our life hellish. Try as I might, I can never get those ghastly images of the second officer's body in flames off my mind or his painful shrieks from my ears. The third engineer's broken jaw and teeth is another gruesome sight and I try my best to avoid steering my eyes in his direction. Since that incident no one has dared to break their laws. No one! Not even Captain! If we need to move from our place for any reason, we raise our hand and take their permission. We *never* stare at them and always cooperate with every single of their demand.

Then be it dancing naked in front of them.

It is the last week of August, and still, there's no news from our company about their intention of paying ransom and getting us released. The leader of the pirates boards our ship at regular intervals and orders the Captain to plead with the company. After his calls he leaves us to the mercy of his heavily guarded companions – some thirty, forty of them at any given time all around the ship who work on twelve hour shifts.

Other than the Captain no one has been allowed to make a call to their family after that first time. I can't say if Aisha is aware of my plight. I had told mom about the hijack on the phone but I'm not sure if they are in talking terms. But what I can say for sure is she'd give a damn about it.

Food and water have become a luxury here. With no fixed timing and served just once in a day we'd devour it in minutes. But as I said earlier, the wait is excruciating. It's almost evening now and still it hasn't arrived.

'Captain!' The distant bellow of one of them makes all of us turn our head to the voice. One of the pirates charges toward him, the heels of his brown boots evoking a clattering sound against the bridge floor.

'*Captain!*' he howls, his raspy voice portending trouble. 'Clearly your fucking company is not interested in the life of the members of the crew, still no news of our money, huh? So now, we have to do something captain. Some of you must…,' he proclaims, removing the gun slung around his shoulder and placing it in front of him, 'DIE!'

There is a collective gasp from all of us. A wave of trepidation sweeps past the bridge. Within seconds the room gets filled with hushed murmurs. I am greeted with frightened looks wherever I look. *Are they serious? Are they really going to kill us?* Anxious faces turn all around and finally settle at Captain for some sort of…*assurance. Please help us, sir.*

'No, no…,' the Captain says, slowly rising to his feet; the burden of expectations weighing down on him. He folds his hands. 'Please, please, don't do any such thing. I'm trying my best to get your money. The company-'

'*Shut up, Captain!*' The pirate takes a step forward and slaps him twice, his hands running back and forth across Captain's face. Three other pirates walk up to him and stand behind, glaring down at Captain. 'You're not trying your best, you bastard; else we would already have got our money…' He draws an ominous sigh and turns toward us, his eyes scanning as if deciding who he would…*kill first.*

'YOU!' he says, pointing at the deck cadet with a scowl. 'Come here. And you, over there…yes you, come out mother fucker. Both of you sitting behind over there, come out, enough of your company's bullshit. When some of you die only then will they understand.' He spoke through gritted teeth and continued running his eyes through us. *Perhaps he isn't done yet...*

My pulse quickens and a cold sweat breaks across my forehead at the sight of his finger. It is pointing at me.

'Hey you, asshole!' I freeze. 'You also, come out now.'

All five of us share petrified looks with each other and then with the Captain before making our way toward them. *We're all gonna die...?* My breathing has grown laborious and I fight the huge lump in my throat. *This can't be happening...*

'Sir, please,' Captain says, his hands back together, 'please don't do this.'

His words barely register. *You can't help us Captain! No one can help us now!* Within seconds my body has grown numb, my blood cold.

The pirate yanks his gun upward and prods its barrel into the Captain's chest with all his force. The Captain staggers to his feet and falls.

'Captain!' he growls. 'Never tell us what we should or shouldn't do, OK. Never tell us!'

A minute later they make us stand in a row. My hands are pulled behind my back and I feel an abrasive rope around them. And then it becomes tight, really tight. Next a soft yet stinking cloth grazes across my face. Then everything goes black.

'Do you have any last wish, you bastards, ha, ha?'

With my hands tied back and eyes pressed close with a black cloth, I hear one of them sneering.

Few minutes earlier with the cold barrel pressed behind our back all five of us were made to disembark the ship. We walked for a few minutes on what felt like soft mud under the directions of a few of the pirates behind us.

Now, standing motionless, I can feel beads of sweat dripping from my forehead. My mouth has gone completely dry. Above us the birds squawk merrily in oblivion to what's happening below them, and there is the sound of waves crashing against the shore to my left. Other than that I can almost hear my heart pounding against my chest. *I'll die in a few minutes...* All those thoughts about Aisha, a divorce with her, the scrambled pieces of Captain's unfinished story flash in my mind. Do they really mean anything now?

It's weird, I thought, *only when you are about to lose your life, you realize the true meaning of it.*

'Nobody has a last wish?' the same pirate says again. 'OK then, be ready to die!'

Behind my back I clench my fists. *So this is it! Goodbye Aisha!*

And then I hear a series of gun-shots.

40. TIME TO GET THE ANSWERS
August 2011, Somewhere in Somalia

Until this ship I'd never heard the sound of a gun-shot. It is terrifying. More so when you can feel it directed at you. But a few shots later I sense something is wrong. There isn't a single bullet that has pierced my flesh. And then I realize it...

They aren't shooting at us. They are firing in the air. It is just a mock execution, perhaps meant to scare us.

'Bastards!' one of them yells. I hear them approaching us; there is the sound of shoes squishing the damp mud below. 'We'll not kill you so easily,' one of them says in a hoarse voice. 'And not now!' he adds.

And then they start hitting us. I wince in pain every time the hard metal strikes my body in hard, crushing blows. It's either a rod or the gun itself. I retract behind slowly with every passing blow and the pirates follow me. Together with my screams I hear the wails of my four other companions beside me. We all plead for them to stop, but they don't. I feel the warm, sticky fluid oozing out through my left elbow. I crash to the ground falling on my back. The blows continue.

'All of you!' one of them screams. 'Go back on your ship and call your home and tell your families to force the company to pay us our money. Tell them that we torture you, we hit you. Tell your families to put pressure on the company, and if they still don't pay ransom, *then* we'll kill you, Okay. No more firing in the air then.'

They continue hitting interspersing the blows with their heaving kicks.

'Okay, do all of you understand?'

'Yes…yes, sir.' All five of us cry in unison.

When we board back our ship and enter the bridge, all heads turn to us. Hands fly to shut gaping mouths and fearful eyes greet us. I can hear a couple of feeble *Thank Gods!*

The pirates had released our hands and removed the black cloth from our eyes on our way to the bridge. All five of us, I notice, have bruises and winced expressions. I have pressed my right hand tight against my left elbow to obviate loss of blood.

The pirates lead us to the satellite phone and ask us to call our families one by one.

'Hey Captain!' one of them growls. 'You also come here and speak to their family and the company.' The Captain skitters toward us. 'And say that we almost killed them today.'

The Captain nods and passes me a faint smile. I can see from his pained expression he is relieved to see all of us alive. I smile back trying my best to hide my pain. He understands, comes closer, and ties a rag around my elbow. Thankfully the pirates say nothing. I resist the urge to embrace him.

After the other four crewmembers were done sobbing and pleading on the phone, it is my turn. Calling Aisha was out of contention. I call my mother. She picks up after three rings and just my *hello* makes her cry. I tag along with her and recount the day's events together with the harrowing images of the last two months. Through her tears she says she's been calling Sahni uncle everyday and following up the case. Before I could say anything else one of them grabs the handset.

'OK, enough, now,' he says. 'Go back to your places.'

Sensing the opportunity I slowly follow the Captain eyeing the vacant spot next to him. I crash on the floor with him on his left and heave a huge sigh. *Time to get the answers to all my questions!*

Although in pain, I want him to complete his story. Next time pirates won't shoot in the air and I don't want to die before I get my answers.

After all, I've been waiting for them for the last two months.

41. THE DIARY
August 2011, Somewhere in Somalia

'Tell me what you want to know,' Captain whispers leaning into me after five minutes.

Things have slowly settled and everyone is back at their place.

I smile despite the pain. 'How did you know I want to ask you something?' I say, cradling my left elbow in my right arm. Thankfully no more blood is oozing out.

He returns the smile. 'Your eyes told me,' he says, 'the way they have been gawking at me for the last two months.'

I chuckle and glance over my shoulder to the right. The pirates are busy smoking marijuana and nattering in their language. Some of the members of our crew are trying to catch some sleep while others are just twiddling around.

'So then tell me,' I say, settling my eyes back at Captain.

'How's the pain?' he says, motioning toward my elbow.

'Manageable,' I say. 'At least now I've something to put my mind to, the pain I mean, better than sitting idle.'

He grins. 'I wish I could have stopped them.'

'Nobody could have, sir,' I say. 'They are ruthless.'

He nods and eyes me intensely. A ghost of a smile plays on his lips. 'So tell me,' he says. 'What do you want to know?'

'Everything!' I reply. 'When these motherfuckers boarded' – I nod toward the pirates – 'you were telling me you signed the divorce papers and left Nagpur forever. So what happened after that? You told me you never met her after your divorce, then why do you still love her? I mean it's been three decades now since that incident. And please sir, please tell me where is your mistake, because honestly, I don't see any. And yeah' - I scratch my eyebrows awkwardly – 'if you loved her so much, then why did you guys not get back together?'

The smile vanishes from his face instantly and gives way to a solemn expression, and very soon a morose countenance takes over. Parallel lines form on his forehead as deep as a fissure and he immerses himself in thoughts. He takes a deep breath and glances away from me. I follow his gaze and wait. Finally after what seems like an eternity, he glances back at me and clears his throat.

'I'll answer your last question first,' he says.

I nod.

'I learnt a few years after my divorce...that...um...' He wipes a little tear forming at the edge of his eyes. '...that...she died.' He looks away.

My eyes widen. There is a prickling sensation at the back of my neck and I cock my head to the other side. I wouldn't say I am completely shocked at the revelation, part of me had anticipated this, but if that was the case, I am more confused now. *Why does he love her then?* I swallow hard and throw an apologetic expression. He sniffles and pulls up a strong face, turning back at me.

'Sir, um...then why do you...'

'Wait a second,' he says, rooting through his navy blue blazer. 'Here, this will answer your other two questions.'

He hands me a diary. In an instant I recognize it. It is the same old, tattered diary I saw on his desk that afternoon. I accept it and wonder how a dirty thing as this will answer any of my questions. He excuses himself for the washroom, not without the permission of the pirates, of course.

I lean back against the wall and gingerly open his diary.

42. SHIKHA'S DIARY
August 2011, Somewhere in Somalia

When I first held the diary, I thought it belonged to the Captain. But instead his wife had written it.

Why has he been in possession of her diary for so long? I jerk off the thought and scan through it. The first entry was made on the tenth of July, 1974. A flowery writing in blue ink greets my eyes.

10ᵗʰ July, 1974

Wow! That's exactly what I feel at the moment. Finally, finally he said those three golden words to me. I had been waiting and waiting, and today when he finally said 'I love you' I've realized there's absolutely nothing else in this world I could ask for.

Saying it with a rose was even better. I completely loved the gesture. Although I must add when he moved closer to me, I did feel nervous, but when his soft lips touched my forehead, I realized what a sinking heart feeling feels like. I huddled my body in his, feeling his breath, and then, damn, came the rain.

Today has to be one of the best days of my life. Hope to see many, many more days like these.

Love you so much Shekhar!

Okay, so the bitch did love him after all. Good to know that. I quickly flick through the pages to find something interesting and more importantly something that answers my questions. As of now there isn't anything noteworthy in them, just some random notes about their dates around the city of Nagpur, how much he loved her, about their orphanage, none of which is new to me. The Captain had already told me the most of it. Still, I can't stop myself from reading each and every word of it.

12ᵗʰ October, 1980

Absolutely nothing could have gone even a shade better today. I got married, on my birthday. When the magistrate called out 'Congrats you are married', I knew it then that my life has changed forever. Oh God, I have always wanted to be Shekhar's wife, even that day, a few years back, when our teacher had asked me. I still remember saying I was Shekhar bhaiya's wife and everyone had burst out laughing. I would always remember that day and then, of course, today.

But who says dreams don't come true, of course they do, if they are pure and straight from the heart. I can never thank the Almighty enough.

Love you so much Shekhar!

'Hey Ronit,' the Captain tousles my hair. 'So where have you reached so far?'

'Oh!' I look up. 'You have been in there a long time.' I nod in the direction of the washroom. 'I've just reached your marriage part.'

'Good.' He plunks down beside me.

I run my eyes quickly through the words. I must admit I am growing damn impatient. Everywhere I can see her thanking him for flowers, for being so loving and supportive, and for understanding her. At one place she even said he *has* to be the best husband in the world. *So then why the divorce...?*

I continue reading.

12ᵗʰ January, 1981

Another of my most special days today - our first quarterly anniversary! And I can't believe Shekhar took it so seriously. From where does he get these beautiful ideas? The roses in the shape of hearts, those wonderful gifts, and, Oh my God, what a beautiful letter it was! How could I ever be so blessed? Perhaps whatever God took from me when I was a child, he's returning a thousand times over.

I loved the way his eyes lit up when I told him I am pregnant. I'm sure he's as thrilled as I am. Hopefully I can give him at least five babies as we planned earlier and live through our dream of a big family.

Love you so much Shekhar!

I turn the pages further. In the following notes she'd written how psyched up both of them were for the pregnancy. She'd written some tentative names of boys and girls, and then if twins, if triplets and so on...I turn the pages quickly. Still nothing. Nothing that would evoke a sigh, pop my eyes out, make my hairs stand, or anything of the ilk. Just the general happy go lucky stories, I found rushing my eyes through.

Just then something caught my eyes.

43. SHIKHA'S DIARY, CONTINUED
August 2011, Somewhere in Somalia

5th February, 1981

For the past few weeks I had a headache. I checked up my temperature regularly, but surprisingly I wasn't down with fever. It somehow went up in the mornings as I woke up and subsided as the day progressed. Thinking of it as a side effect of pregnancy, I let it go. But then for the last few days the pain had increased substantially, so today, I thought of visiting a doctor and getting a check-up done. At first I thought I should wait for Shekhar till the weekend, but then decided against it.

After hearing my symptoms, the doctor did a few tests, and then eyed me gloomily. I asked him if everything is alright, but his expression offered otherwise.

As I write this, I shudder even to think why all this happened.

I have a tumour in my brain. The doctor told me it's incurable and no treatment can save me. I have one or two months left.

Maximum three.

10th February, 1981

Today is the worst day of my life. After my first visit few days back, I visited another doctor, and then another. But my worst fear was confirmed when the results were the same. Instead they told me another thing – I should get an abortion done. Being just two months pregnant now, there is no way I could be living for that long – six, seven more months - they said. So after contemplating it for the past two days, I got it done.

My heart is heavy and there's absolutely nothing I can do to stop my tears. I can't breathe, I can't move. I don't know what I should do. I don't even want to say anything to Shekhar about this. I don't know what he'll do to himself. But then I have to tell him someday...

I love you so much Shekhar, please, please help me.

13ᵗʰ February, 1981

Shekhar should never find out what happened to me. If he does, what will he do without me a few months from now? I'm sure he'll never move on and spend the rest of his life alone. He'll be shattered and devastated and I can't let that happen to him.

So I have decided something. I will not tell about my disease to anyone. No one! Not even Swati. But that's not the hard part. I have decided something else as well.

I have to make him fall out of love with me.

15ᵗʰ February, 1981

Today we had our first fight. I had placed my abortion papers with some of his papers in the bed-side drawer. I had hoped he'll definitely notice them. And thankfully he did. I'd also thought about the reason I'd give him when asked for it. He is sure to hate me for it.

Although I should feel miserable about it, but instead, I'm happy, happy for Shekhar. This is the first of my many steps. I still have a long way to go. By the time I'm taking my last breath, he should hate me completely so he never thinks about me for the rest of his life.

Sorry Shekhar, I love you so much but I have to do this.

09th *March, 1981*

Oh God, I hate myself for calling his Baba and him a loser. I'm so, so sorry Shekhar. I didn't mean a word. I hope I could tell you this but unfortunately I can't. Please forgive me. You are my hero, the best person I've ever known, and I have such deep respect for your Baba. I don't need money Shekhar; I don't even care about it. I just want to live with you. But as simple as that sounds, it's not possible.

I wish I could stop fighting with you, hug you and cry with you that our relationship wouldn't last long. But I can't get selfish. I have to make you hate me. I have to live the last phase of my life alone, so that you can live peacefully after me.

Once again, I'm sorry Shekhar, I'm very sorry. I love you so much, please forgive me.

26th *March, 1981*

Oh Shekhar, really sorry for not being a good wife, for not fulfilling my duty. I do realize I don't cook for you and I'm not carrying out any household chores. I'm really sick, my head is throbbing with pain, and I feel so dizzy. I know you think that I'm faking this, but trust me my love, I'm not. I love you so much and would love to take care of you. I'm missing our meals together, in the same plate, you feeding me, I feeding you, talking and laughing for hours.

I don't mean a word of what I said today. I know you didn't marry me to have your food cooked and have someone to look after your house. I purposely said those words to instigate you. I'm so sorry Shekhar, so, so, sorry.

Love you so much Shekhar.

09th April, 1981

How could I forget Rajiv and Swati's wedding? Oh God, I'm such a fool. She did come a few days earlier and handed me the card. I remember now, she was so excited.

Probably the memory loss associated with my disease is finally coming to play. My doctor had told me about it, but I never agreed. How could I be forgetting things? Perhaps I am now.

I wish I could have gone to her wedding with Shekhar. Swati would have made such a beautiful bride. Sorry Shekhar, you missed your best friend's wedding because of me. And please Shekhar, please do not say I'm embarrassed in your company. I'm so proud of you and our relationship.

Love you Shekhar, love you so much.

10th April, 1981

Oh God, where have I kept the money? Of course I remember spending some of it on my medicines and in the clinic, but what about the rest. What is happening to me? Why am I forgetting so much?

And I hate it when you yell at me Shekhar. I wish I could tell you that, but I can't. I'm sorry Shekhar for everything. I don't know what's happening to me. I'm so, so sorry. Please forgive me.

17th April, 1981

I have to get separated from him before he finds out about my disease. Otherwise my plan will fail. So while I still appear normal, I'll have to divorce him. It'll bring an enormous amount of pain to both of us, but, in the end I know it'll be the best decision. At least for Shekhar.

I can't get selfish here and I'll rather choose dying alone in pain on my bed over a bereaved Shekhar for decades to come. I'm left with just a few weeks anyway whereas Shekhar has his whole life in front of him.

So, right here, on my bed, amidst tears in my eyes, I've decided I'll end this.

I'll divorce him. Tomorrow.

18th April, 1981

I have succeeded in what I wanted to achieve, but yet, I have failed. I have lost the most important person of my life and I'm all alone here in this house. There is no one to wipe my tears and there is no one to tell me that what I did was right. But I had to do this, I had to divorce him. Although I'm left with just a few weeks, every day without him will be a lifetime.

But at least now I can die peacefully, feeling safe that Shekhar hates me and has left me. I hope he finds someone else as wonderful as him.

I don't know what made him think I was having an extra-marital affair. But in a way it was good. He'll hate me all the more and erasing my memories from his heart would be easier.

Goodbye Shekhar, I would miss you a lot in these last days of mine. Hope you get success and happiness wherever you go. And may you fulfil your Baba's dream.

Love you forever.

44. THE ADVICE
August 2011, Somewhere in Somalia

I keep the diary aside as I can't read any further. My throat has become as tight as metal, and in a matter of seconds, tears have filled my eyes. Suddenly everything is crystal clear.

Why he still loves her so much...?

Why does he think it was entirely his mistake...?

What he meant when he said I didn't understand her after marriage...?

All of it made perfect sense now, and I'm amazed by their breathtaking love story. She could have told him about his disease, *but yet...* She could have chosen to spend her remaining days with him, *but yet...* The Captain could have moved on and carried with his life, *but yet...*

With tears in my eyes I turn to face Captain. 'Sorry sir,' I say, sniffling. 'I'm really sorry for what happened.' I hear my voice crack and my hand reaches to wipe my eyes.

Captain smiles. His forehead creases as he looks up at me. 'So now you know, huh?' he says, his voice soft as feather.

I nod and run an arm over my running nose. 'When did um...you find out?'

Captain takes a deep breath. 'I was in Bombay those days,' he replies, looking in the distance. 'After my divorce I had enrolled in an Indian Shipping company. A month later Rajiv met me there and told me Shikha had passed away. He collected her belongings and passed them on to me.'

Tears slowly find their way out of his eyes and he cups his face in his hands. After wiping his face, he looks at me plaintively. 'You know, he told me later he hadn't read the diary, else he would never have handed it to me so Shikha could have succeeded in her plan. However I was so glad I read it, and then...I think I fell in love with her all over again. I have never forgiven myself...' He trails off and when I look at him again I can surely say I have never seen someone cry like that. His quick guttural gasps are tempered with the heaving motion of his chest and what began as a demure sob soon turns into a high- pitched wail. It is so infectious that I can't suppress the flow of tears of my own. I can honestly say I've never been so overwhelmed with someone else's story.

A few heads turn toward us but we don't care. The pirates aren't bothered either.

I let the silence take over our conversation for a while and relive those days, those fights, and arguments with Aisha. The affliction it brought to me is nothing as compared to what the Captain had to go through.

'Sorry sir,' I say again after a few minutes, rubbing my eyes. 'I'm very sorry for your loss.'

He waves his hand. 'No, it's alright,' he says, slightly composed now. 'You know normally I never discuss all this with anyone. Quite simply they don't care; neither do I feel like telling them anyway. No one has the time to listen to an old man's story. But when I see young people like you, making a mockery of true love, my heart cries. I think about my Shikha and remember what all she did for me. True love still exists in this world. You know she could have been selfish and told me about it, at least she would have had me in her last moments. But instead she chose to die alone so that I could lead a better life. It pains me so much to think that during her last days, there was no one to look after her. No one! She died alone, battling all the pain, only for me...' He takes a deep shaky breath and a fresh set of tears emerge from his eyes. 'I hate myself for it, for what I did to her in her last days. I yelled at her all the time for her lack of responsibility, I shouted at her telling her to stop feigning illness, but she was...she was actually sick. I shouted at her for forgetting things, but it was her *disease* that was doing all that to her. I even maligned her for having an extra-marital *affair*. God only knows how she would have felt about my accusation...'

He wraps his arms around his legs and tucks his head between his knees. The slow motion of his chest manifests his sobs. A few minutes later, he lifts his head and turns to me, his eyes dark and pudgy from the tears.

'And look at you guys today, what you have made of love. You were madly in love with your wife but due to trivial reasons you want to divorce her. You think you can live happily after that?' When my blank expression had nothing to offer, he continues. 'Without my Shikha you think I have ever been happy. You know even after my divorce, before I found out all this, I cried every day. I still missed her. I still loved her. And then later when I had cognizance about her plan, I was proud of the fact that there once was such a wonderful person who loved me so much. That feeling has made me live my life so far. In the end that's all that matters: the feeling of being in love and the joy of being loved back. Nothing else.'

'I understand sir…,' I say, hesitating, observing the sincerity in his words. I allow my mind to drift in the thoughts of Aisha. 'I think…I think I still love Aisha, sir,' I say, struck by the realization. 'But um…I don't know what to do.'

The Captain nods but says nothing for a few minutes as if getting himself back together. 'Look,' he finally says, rubbing his eyes and scooting closer. 'If you have learnt anything from my story, just remember there is nothing better in this world than living your life with the person you love. In my case it didn't last long, but yet, I cherish every single moment of my life I spent with her. You are fortunate enough that you can make it last a lifetime. Do it. Be the best husband you can be. Tell her that you love her, *everyday*. Make her feel special. Throw a few surprises at her every now and then. And then you'll see how blissful your own life will get. Remember women are always emotionally stronger than men. We need them more than they need us. Give your love one last chance and you'll be amazed by the joy and contentment it'll bring you. Don't make the same mistake I did. I doubted my love. You don't do that; hear out her part of the story. Maybe she's right, but in either case, sort it out. Else three decades later you'll be sitting on some ship like this and doling out your own life story to one of your juniors,' he smiles.

I smile back. 'Right sir,' I say. 'I'll think about it.'

45. THREE MONTHS LATER...
November 2011, Somewhere in Somalia

Oh, I love Aisha. I really do.

Five months of separation from her has rekindled my feelings for her. I miss her and find myself reliving those moments with her when all was well with the world. I miss her smile, the lilt in her voice, those pretty eyes, and sometimes, our futile arguments.

Captain was right – I wasn't supportive enough. In fact I never understood her after marriage and always supported my family even when I knew they were at fault. I haven't been a good husband, now I can say that for sure.

Whenever I'm back home, *if I'm back home,* I'll give our marriage one last chance. This much I have to do; the Captain's story has inspired me to do at least that.

But then again, an ominous *if* hangs in the air. Honestly, I can't be sure if we'll manage to survive this ordeal. The worst part of our suffering is the wait. *That* is killing us slowly. The enormous mental strain, of course, is another factor. It's been five months now and we continue to huddle against each other on the bridge with more than two dozen ghoulish looking pirates staring down at us with their guns.

Add to it the frequent hitting. Yes, they beat us every now and then whenever they get drunk. They pick us out at random and then unleash their fury at us forcing the Captain to call the company and plead with them for the ransom. Other than that they frequently perform mock executions – like they did last time, but you can never be sure about it, and that's what makes it insanely traumatizing – and crew lock downs. Once in a while they handpick one or two of us and push us separately in a common toilet or a duct space with no access to food, water, or electricity for as long as a week.

But yet, the company doesn't care. I have come to realize that the value of a human life is nothing, more so, when the life in question is that of an Indian. Had it been the Europeans or Americans, their government would have intervened and exercised their clout to free their fellow countrymen. On the other hand the Indian government has arrested scores of pirates in Indian waters which has further exacerbated our misery. The pirates are using us as bargaining chips even after they receive their ransom to get their people released.

And it is this realization, coupled by various others, that is killing us every day.

The pirates haven't allowed us to call our families either after that day of mock execution. I'm dying to speak to Aisha just once, I don't know if she's even aware of my plight.

The only silver lining in the cloud has been the Captain who is seated beside me. He has been exhorting me to try to save our relationship before even considering a divorce. And I have agreed. Yes, I have. As soon as I'm out of here, I'll meet Aisha and request her to give us one last shot.

Of course, even then if things don't work out between us, it's better for us to part our ways. But this much is sure that I won't beg her and plead with her to take me back.

I have my male ego intact after all.

46. SIX MONTHS LATER...
Somewhere in Somalia, May 2012

To hell with my male ego!
I love her and I'll do *anything* so she takes me back. I'll beg her, I'll plead with her and then I'll beg more until she agrees. I just can't live without her.

In case you are still wondering what made the neurotic in me change it's the time that has worked its magic. Yeah, that's what it does to you. It's been almost a year in captivity and as much time away from Aisha. Only when you lose a person do you realize their true worth in your life. Though I haven't lost her, just yet, I can't be sure if I still have her either.

I've been thinking all these months when I was home I hated her for all her shortcomings but never loved her for her virtues. And here, it's the other way round. I've learnt something about human beings while dawdling away my time here. We always judge people by their negativities and never by their moralities. At home I never saw Aisha' love, warmth, and the sacrifices she made for me. Instead I only saw her arguments with my family, and of course, the devil in her. I can't even begin to express how much I hate myself for that now. And that, I believe, has reinforced my feelings for her.

Moreover, the Captain's story has reinstated my belief in love. Hardly an hour passes when my mind doesn't drift in

Aisha's thoughts. These last six months have made me realize what a blunder I would have made had I divorced her. In a way, I think, it was good our ship got hijacked. Had it not been for the pirates, I would have been home long time back, and divorced Aisha. Whatever happens, surely, happens for the best.

But that's not all that I think about here. Of course, I apprehend Aisha would have her own take of all this and if I can think of a divorce, why not her? But I sincerely hope she doesn't think that I have forgotten her. The fact that I haven't been able to call her and she's not in talking terms with my mother has only bolstered these negative thoughts. *What if she thinks I have moved on...? What if she has moved on...? What if she has found another guy...?*

The last few months I've been battling these thoughts out of my head. But that's the thing - I have nothing else to do here. I just sit here in the same position day in day out along with the other members of the crew, my mind always a whirlpool of thoughts.

Meanwhile life here continues to be miserable. In fact, things have gotten worse. Due to the mental strain and lack of food and water, diseases are afflicting members of the crew, and medical help isn't forthcoming. A few of us have stomach infections and one deck crew member has lost his eyesight. Our chief engineer is an asthmatic and he consumed his inhaler two months back. Every breath is a struggle for him and the sound of his wheezing doesn't implore the pirates to call for a doctor. I can't be sure if he'll make it.

The Captain has suffered two strokes in the last six months, but again, no medical help arrived. We all were by his side helping him in whatever little way we could.

One of us has even committed suicide. Apparently unhinged from stress and the affliction of waiting, the fourth officer rushed toward the bridge wings and jumped in the water last month. Nobody stopped him.

Perhaps, I think, he made a better choice.

It is the last week of May and much to our consternation we see more than fifty pirates boarding our ship through the gangway. My first thought is that they'll be transferring all of us somewhere else, but when they tell us that today we'll be going home, a wave of euphoria washes over us. At first none of us believe them dismissing it as another of their mock acts. But when they begin packing their weapons in duffel bags and tell us we are free to move, reality slowly sinks in. I burst out in tears in anticipation of meeting with Aisha again. The Captain smiles and embraces me tightly in his arms.

'You know what you need to do now,' he whispers in my ear.

'Of course sir,' I reply, wiping my tears. 'Thank you so much for sharing your story with me.'

He nods and ruffles my hair.

One by one we all hug and congratulate each other. *The company has finally agreed to pay the ransom!*

An hour later we see a helicopter approaching the ship. The whir of its blades is deafening and we press our hands against our ears. It hovers above the ship at a height of at least hundred metres. All loose items on deck scatter with the column of air under it. A few bags of canvas are dropped on the ship's deck from the helicopter and then it vanishes into the overcast sky leaving behind a trail of smoke. The pirates scamper toward the bags and begin counting the money. Fifteen minutes later, together with the bags and their weapons, all of them disembark the ship. This confuses us as without any fuel and supplies it is impossible to sail back to India. After receiving their ransom they should have at least helped us with that. However we know our priority should be to leave Somalia first lest another pirate gang hijacks us.

The ship's engines are started immediately to exit Somalia's territorial waters and soon we begin sailing in a south-easterly direction toward Mumbai port.

After a while, the ship's engines break down. Without running for eleven months and with no maintenance this was not unexpected. Luckily a naval ship not too far from us rescues us and they tell us they are en route to Mombasa in Kenya which would take two days. Medical help is rendered to us, and we inform our families of our freedom.

On arrival at Mombasa our company arranges tickets for us to fly to Mumbai. Finally after eleven months and five days, our ordeal is over.

But my next ordeal begins. Aisha, I'm coming...

47. JOE SINGH'S ADVICE, AGAIN
30th May 2012, Mumbai

At the Chhatrapati Shivaji International Airport of Mumbai, we have to fight our way through a scrum of media persons and journalists.

'How was the entire experience of living as hostages?' asks one journalist.

'Were any of you physically hurt or tortured?' asks another.

'How are all of you feeling now?'

I quickly trail behind the Captain who leads me to the exit area. I don't have even a minute to waste and I guess the Captain could sense that. We leave members of our crew with a blizzard of questions from the journalists.

How are you feeling now? Can a question get any lamer?

Outside, Captain hugs me. We exchange our telephone numbers and address. He urges me to visit him at his place with Aisha once everything is settled.

'Of course, sir,' I say. 'I promise.'

Next, I take a taxi straight to Joe Singh's home. Perhaps it'll be a good idea to speak to him first before facing Aisha.

'Holy shit! What the hell happened?' Joe Singh screams at my sight in front of his door.

Of course, with my long, unkempt hair, and straggly beard I expected him to be shocked.

'Can I come in first,' I ask.

He moves aside, his mouth wide open as I struggle with my luggage. His house smells the way a typical north Indian's house would. The smell of paranthas waft toward the living room and I find myself basking in it. How much I missed good Indian food in the last eleven months?

'In case you don't realize,' he says with a confused look, 'I'm still waiting.'

'Our ship got hijacked,' I say, throwing the luggage in one corner and crashing on the black rexine couch.

'Oh God, when?' His hands fly to his mouth and he plunks down beside me. 'And why did no one tell me about it?'

'That's because they didn't allow us to call, you slob.'

'Oh, okay,' he says, making a face while poking his finger in my rough, dishevelled hair.

They are smelly, sticky, and I do realize I desperately need a haircut.

'Tell me everything, will you?'

As if I have a choice. I tell him everything right since the day the pirates boarded, their harassing, mock executions, crew lock downs, and I couldn't stop myself from sharing Captain's story as well. In between, his maid offered paranthas, and I devour at least a dozen of them while recounting my last year.

'My God!' he says when I'm done. 'That's an incredibly sad story, dude.'

I nod.

'Okay, wait,' I say, gulping down the curd I was offered along. I must admit that has to be the most delicious meal

I ever had. 'Which sad story are you referring to here – the pirates' or Captains'?'

'The Captain's story, of course.'

I jerk the curd bowl in his face and his beard gets smeared by the last bits of it. 'I almost died that day and you find Captain's story sadder, you psycho.'

He runs a hand through his beard and smiles. We both shake our head and say nothing. Instead we just look at each other and share another smile. For whatever reason we high-five. I can't escape the thought it's been a year I shared such a moment with my best friend. Nothing can be more important in life than friends. No – wait - wife is the most important.

His maid returns with a despondent look and asks me if I need any more paranthas.

'Only two more,' I say. I hate that smirk on her face before she marches down the hallway toward the kitchen. 'And another bowl of curd, please,' I call out to her.

'You know,' he resumes, 'he's so right when he says you can't forget your first love. Seriously, you can't. Maybe a woman can, but never a man.'

'Joe,' I say for a change, 'how the hell do you even know that. You've never been in love, man. And how do you know so much about women anyway. This is something that has always intrigued me.'

'Oh!' he leans back in his seat. 'Yeah...well...'

I eye him askance. 'Joe, what are you hiding?'

He takes a deep breath and then looks away. 'Nothing... really.'

'Joe Singh!' I say, widening my eyes at him.

'OK..., well, there's something...I've hidden from you.'

'What?' I scooted closer to him. For a moment I forgot the purpose of my visit here.

'OK...,' he looks away again. 'The thing is I've been in love with a woman for the last seven years.'

'Okay.'

'Um...actually...she is Chinese,' he says slowly.

'What?'

'Yeah...and I met her in a bar in China.'

'Go on.'

'You know one of *those* bars.'

'What?' I shot up. Even the last two paranthas the maid got me a minute ago didn't interest me anymore. 'She is a prostitute?'

'No, not exactly,' he countered. 'She just works there.'

'So she is a bar dancer.'

'No, damn it.' He hurls a cushion at me. 'I said she just works there.'

'So she's a bar dancer cum prostitute, okay, got it.'

He makes a face.

'Anyway, so what about her?' I ask.

'Well,' he says with a smile, scratching his beard. 'I've been madly in love with her ever since I met her and want to get married to her. You know we'd been dating each other for a long time and then we broke up last year, again patched up and again broke up, and then one more time this year. She is a typical woman and pesters me so much, yet I can't stop loving her. That's why I always sail in Chinese waters, so I can be with her most of the time. Being with her has made me realize what a woman really wants. And well, that's how I know so much about women.'

I am stunned. I'm not even hungry anymore. So this is the reason he knows so much about women, something that has been plaguing me for the last so many years. *And I've been following all his insanely advices about women...* No wonder, my marriage has fallen apart.

'So let me get this again,' I say, my hands stretched out. 'Being with a Chinese bar dancer cum prostitute you learnt what a woman wants and *that's* how you know so much about women...I mean, wow!'

'Yes!' he says. 'So what man, love is blind. You forgot your own time. You fell in love with our enemy's sister, Priyanka's sister, he, he...'

'So...you do believe in love then.'

'Of course, man. It's the most beautiful thing in the whole world.'

'So then why have you been hiding this all this while?'

'Because...dude, it's embarrassing.'

I shake my head in disbelief. 'Can you even imagine what sort of children both of you will give birth to? Can you not see it? Chinese eyes and a turban on top, Oh God, Joe, buddy, you are amazing!'

He says nothing.

I know what I have to do now. If Joe Singh can be in love with a Chinese...whatever and still can't get her off his head, then I will never be able to forget Aisha.

I leave his house and run with all brute force toward Aisha's place.

Ten minutes later, I am still running.

Why the hell did I not take his car?

48. SORRY AISHA, SORRY PRIYANK
30th May 2012, Mumbai

I bring Joe Singh's car to a screeching halt outside Aisha's house. *Why the hell was I running if I could drive?*

That definitely had to be Bollywood's melodramatic effect. As sense had dawned on me I'd sprinted back to Joe Singh's place, crawled behind the steering wheel of his car, and then drove at breakneck speed.

Now, here I am, outside the door of Aisha's place in Bandra. A sinking sensation forms in the pit of my stomach as I imagine what her reaction would be. *Would she be happy to see me? Would she fall in my arms? Would she take me back in her life or...would she kick me out her house?*

I knock.

After a minute, for what seemed like an hour, the door creaks open. It's my handsome brother-in-law Priyank. He looks dashing in his sky blue chinos and um...pink shirt that is rolled behind to expose his fair arms.

I clear my throat. 'Hey Priyank!'

'Oh! Look who's here,' he says; his voice cold and surly. 'The mystery man is back. We thought you got lost.'

'Actually my ship got...um...never mind. Is Aisha around?'

He raised his eyebrows. 'Why do you want to see her now, after such a long time?'

'Please.'

'And what's with all that hair and beard,' he says. His nose crinkles to form a frown. 'You like *Devdas* of some shady movie.'

'Please, can I see Aisha?'

He hesitates for a moment. 'OK, come in,' he offers and moves aside.

I settle on the L-shaped sofa in the living room. Memories of that day when Priyank had caught us came rushing back. We were so much in love those days and life seemed just the perfect place to be in. And now, everything had changed. Only if Aisha could give me one last chance, I'll restore the old times. I'll become the best husband in the world, the most caring and supportive husband, even better than the Captain.

Aisha emerges slowly from her bedroom. With a loose Nike pyjama and a sky blue top she looks even more beautiful than the first time I saw her.

'Hi there,' I say and rise on my feet slowly. I do realize hugging her wouldn't be a good idea now.

Her face is expressionless. She definitely doesn't look pleased to see me here.

'Hmm...so what brings you to Mumbai after a year?'

She crosses her arms against her chest, and leans against the wall beside her.

'Can I give you a hug?'

'No, not at all,' she says and then looks away. 'It took one year for you to realize that you have a wife.'

'Aisha, I'm sorry, really sorry, you know my sh...'

'Just get the hell out of here, Ronit!' she says stretching her arms and nodding toward the door.

'At least let me say what I have to.'

'I don't care what you have to say, Ronit.' She took a step forward. 'When I needed you, you weren't even there and now you have suddenly realized you need me. Where were you all this while, huh?'

'Aisha, my ship got hijacked.'

'Oh,' she says, biting her lower lip. 'Really?'

'You think I would lie about a thing like that, Aisha,' I say and walk toward her. 'We were under their captivity for more that eleven months. In fact I returned to India this morning. Don't you see my condition?' I point toward my beard and hair.

'Why couldn't you at least call?' she says and retracts back.

'The pirates never allowed us to, Aisha. Only my mom knew about it but you guys don't even...never mind.'

I move closer again and hold her shoulders. Priyank dawdles a few metres away from us to monitor our conversation. Perhaps he thinks the hooligan in me would harm his sister.

Aisha stands motionless and doesn't let go off my arm. We glance at each other occasionally feeling the awkwardness of the situation.

'So? What now Ronit? Why are you here?'

'I love you Aisha, I really do. I'm so, so sorry for what I did to you. Being away from you in the last year has made me realize how much you mean to me. Can you give me one last chance to improve my mistakes?'

She doesn't reply. Instead she walks away from me across the hall toward the couch. She sits on it and buries her face in her hands.

'Why?' she says, looking at me. 'Why should I give you another chance? You left me when I needed you the most.'

'Because I have changed, Aisha.' I walk toward her. 'And because things have changed. I spoke to mom and Priya has moved out as well. Things have finally settled in her family. She won't trouble you anymore.'

'So?'

I drop to my knees and place my hands on her laps. 'Come on Aisha, you know I love you so much.'

Priyank sneers at me from behind her. *Why can't he leave us alone?*

'Please forgive me Aisha.'

'Why...why should I forgive you?'

I close my eyes and remember something. 'Because I love you a lot and I'll become exactly what you want me to become Aisha,' I say. 'I'll be a caring, supportive, and loving husband who doesn't buy you gold biscuits so it can be a *fair investment* for me. Instead I'll shower gifts on you and flatter you with a lot of surprises. I'll be courteous and polite, would love you, and be kind like I was before marriage. I'll be sensitive and listen to your problems attentively and then solve it and not give you the crap that I won't interfere in you women. I'll spend maximum time with you and next time my sister is rude to you, I'll stand by you.'

Thankfully, this time the tune of 'stand by me' didn't play in my mind.

'I'll respect you, your feelings and your desires, and then

fulfill each one of them. I will understand the sacrifices you have made for me by leaving your family. I'll be a good friend, a good companion, and most importantly a man. I'll be a good listener, be warm, sympathetic, attentive, funny, tender, tolerant, understanding, courageous, dependable.'

Neither did 'Rahul Dravid' come to my mind.

'I'll be passionate, compassionate and honest. I'll help you in the kitchen and not merely order what I want to eat. And after my meals, I'll pick up my own dishes and keep them in the sink not before spraying some water over them. I won't put my wet towel on the bed and certainly not on the floor. My shoes would lie neatly in the shoe rack and the socks would go in the laundry. I will not throw my clothes on the bed and expect you or my mother to put it in the wardrobe for me. I'll eat whatever you cook for me, enjoy it and then compliment you for it, as at least you are trying.

'You can wake up any time in the morning, take a shower when you want, wear any clothes in the house. Other than that I will compliment you frequently as I did before marriage and not give you any stress.'

She stares at me and her mouth is wide open. 'You remembered all that I said?'

Priyank comes forward, his face puckered in contempt, and sits beside her.

'Yes Aisha, I remember each and every word.'

Slowly a faint smile forms at the corner of her lips.

I hold her hand and smile back. 'Would you please come home with me?'

Much to my chagrin, she hesitates. She looks at Priyank who offers a shrug in return.

'Please Aisha give me one last chance, I'll do anything you want me to.'

'Anything?' she eyes me skeptically and then looks at Priyank.

I nod.

Oh God, I have a bad feeling about this.

Rightly so, half an hour later, Aisha and Priyank are shoving up a gel inside me, of course, from behind. They tell me it's a mixture of garlic, red chilies, and pepper.

The next instant I scream my lungs out and wriggle in pain on the floor. My butt is burning and I have never experienced such excruciating pain in my life.

Oh, I hate Joe Singh. I hate that bastard. Why the hell did he invent this stupid game?

One piece of advice, though. Please, never, ever try this at home!

EPILOGUE

A year has passed and the Captain's words have never left my mind.

It's not too hard to keep a woman happy. All they want is our love, care, support, and apparently a good ear.

It took me almost a year under the captivity of pirates, and the story of a lifetime to understand that, but still, as they say, better late than never.

We're more in love with each other than ever before. Thankfully my sister Priya is back with her husband, and peace is restored both in her and our home. I spend enough time with Aisha and never hang out with my friends or cousins alone. A few days back I asked her to celebrate our wedding anniversaries quarterly and she was thrilled.

'Where do you get such wonderful ideas from?' she asked me.

I smiled and replied, 'Well, I'm a romantic, what can I say?'

She loves surprises and I love surprising her with gifts, and of course, flowers. Captain was right - there is an unimaginable affinity between women and flowers. The hug that I get in return and the geniality that follows for the next few days makes the effort worthwhile a ten times over.

Oh yeah, and did I tell you about Priyank?

She got, I mean, he got married last month. No, seriously. Though the woman (yes woman) he got married to is – well, how do I put it – strange. She looks…manly, if you know what I mean. On his marriage day, my handsome brother-in-law appeared…scared. God bless that idiot.

And Joe Singh is getting married to that Chinese…whatever. He's madly in love with her, he tells me whenever we meet, and cannot imagine his life without her. Last when we met he told me he's writing a book from all his experiences, *How to keep your woman happy – and stop that blah, blah, blah.*

I am *never* going to read it.

Now, I am in Mumbai and we are on our way toward Captain's house in Andheri. I want Aisha to meet the Captain and vice-versa. Moreover I want to see a picture of Shikha Ma'am – the woman who reaffirmed my belief in love without even meeting me.

And yeah, there's another thing I must tell you. I've realized now that love can definitely last forever, even if you marry your love.

*****

www.ingramcontent.com/pod-product-compliance
Lightning Source LLC
Chambersburg PA
CBHW052028020726
47501CB00004B/1300